D1519825

ONE SPRING DAY

Geralyn Vilar

All The Best!
Geralyn Vilar

Although inspired by a true story, the characters and events in this book are fictitious and are a product of the authors imagination

To Natalie, for her inspiration.

To my husband, David, for his love and

encouragement.

To my sons Alexander Garcia & Anthony Casale

for always encouraging me to follow my dreams.

Chapters

PROLOGUE

It was only 7pm and the night air was colder than he could recall, 17 degrees with howling winds. He crawled into one of the black plastic bags he brought with him and tried to make a tent out of the other. This make-shift tent shielded only his head and neck. Some of the snow had turned to ice and even with the down coat and his expensive gloves, he was freezing. He felt hot and cold all over and the constant cough gave him little rest. Weak and exhausted, he slipped in and out of consciousness. He was dreaming, an angelic voice in the distance seemed to call to him but he was unable to respond. The voice was overshadowed by sirens.

"Where am I? I'm so cold", he said, shaking and coughing violently.

"You're in the emergency room", the nurse said as she covered him with another warm blanket.

"What's wrong with me"?

"We don't know yet". His memory was lacking from the episodes of delirium. He looked around the room. There was equipment everything and he was hooked up to all of it. Multiple bags of IV fluids, a heart monitor, nasal oxygen, a pulse oximeter, and an automatic blood pressure cuff.

"Why don't I remember coming to the hospital"?

"Your fever was so high that you were delirious. You are doing much better today. I assume you're homeless...living on the street"?
"How do you know that"? he asked with surprise.
"A young woman was walking home and heard you coughing and moaning. She called 911. The EMT's said they found you in a plastic bag behind some bushes. That woman may have saved your life".

It was all he could do to concentrate. He had been sick for a while. The nights are so cold this time of year and the snow and ice had made it unbearable to sleep. He was warming up now and finally drifting off to sleep. He awoke the next day bathed and wearing a clean hospital

gown. This was quite a relief after weeks of

living on the street and wearing the same clothes

day in and day out. As sick as he was, he felt

calm and peaceful, something he had not felt

since that horrible day three weeks ago. There

was a quiet tap on his hospital room door. "Hi,

I'm Sara she said as she walked toward him. Are

you Jonathan Donnelly"?

"Yes", he answered.

"I wanted to check on you", her voice

sounded familiar.

"Check on me"? He was puzzled. "Do I

know you"?

"No, we never met. Last night while I was

walking home from the grocery store. I heard

your relentless coughing. You didn't respond

when I approached you and asked if you were

okay.   .... so, I called 911".

"I didn't respond to you"? He said with a

flirtatious chuckle.... "I must have r e a l l y been

sick".

"Well, thank you". she said with a smile.

He could see that she was blushing.

Sara was a beautiful woman, tall and slim with

long brown hair and hazel eyes. Her smile lit up

the room. She wore a sable cashmere walking

coat that was unbuttoned, revealing a navy dress

that accentuated her figure. "Please...sit down",

he motioned to a chair beside his bed "and feel

free to take off your coat. It's much too warm in

here for a winter coat". She took him up on his

offer and as she sat, she said, "I'm glad you're

feeling better today. Do they know what caused

you to be unresponsive last night"?

"I had a high fever. I think they said I have pneumonia and that I was dehydrated. I'm not really sure.... I was so out of it last night. Thank you for calling 911. The nurse said that you may have saved my life".

"Anyone would have done the same. I'm just glad you are alright".

"Look at the time, she said as she glanced at her watch. I'm going to be late for work".

"Where do you work"?

"I work as a law clerk just a few blocks from here". Brains and beauty all wrapped up in one package, he thought.

"Your parents must be proud of you".

"They are, thank you but I must get going".

"Would you consider coming by for another visit"?

"We'll see". she said with a smile as she walked out the door.

Her day started with sort of an obligatory visit to a stranger and in just a few minutes, that stranger felt connected to her as if he were a part of her. She tried to shake it off. After all, she knew nothing about him, and he was quite flirtatious. I won't go back, she decided. He's fine and that is all I need to know. She exited the elevator and left the building. The air had an icy chill that felt like snow was approaching soon. The sky was bright blue with not a cloud in sight. Street signs were swaying as the wind shifted. She started to shiver but didn't notice because at that moment, everything seemed brighter and more alive than ever before.

After three days, Jonathan was giving up on the thought of ever seeing this mystery women again. He was feeling stronger and would be discharged in a few days. The coughing was at a minimum and most of the machines were gone. Sara captivated his thoughts each day...her beauty and intelligence were remarkable. I should have asked for her number. But then, I have nothing to offer her. I can't even afford to buy her a cup of coffee. Who am I kidding? What would she want with me? It's best that she didn't come back.

No matter how she tried, she couldn't stop thinking about him. She replayed their brief meeting over and over in her mind. Jonathan is very attractive and well spoken. He is the sort of guy you would expect to see working at the law firm. Intelligent and sure of himself, yet, she had the distinct impression that he was homeless, living on the streets. This doesn't make sense.... maybe, I'll go back and see him.

It had been 4 days since they met. Jonathan had resigned himself to the fact that he would never see her again. He was seated in a chair, reading, in the back corner of the room away from direct view of the door. Tap tap tap, "may I come in"? He recognized that familiar voice and was thrilled.

"Sara, what a pleasant surprise. Come in".

"How are you feeling"?

"So much better".

"Well you look great".

He laughed. "I look great? I'm in a hospital

gown, not really my best look. I'm so glad you came by".

"Fair enough, she said with a nod. May I sit"?

"Of course, I would get up and give you my chair, but you might get a view of more than you bargained for. This gown is open in the back". They both laughed out loud. Charming and funny she thought.

"Jonathan I was thinking about the night I found you. You were really sick. If you don't mind my asking, why were you out on such a cold night"?

"Unfortunately, he said with hesitation and shame, as of three weeks ago, I have been homeless".

"Homeless???? She exclaimed. So, she

<u>was</u> right, he is homeless.   There was silence for what seemed an eternity. Jonathan, may I ask you a question"?

"Sure".

"You seem intelligent and sure of yourself.........why are you living on the street... I mean, what happened to you"?

"That's a long story", he said shaking his head in dismay.

"Well, I have about an hour before I have to be at work. Will that be enough time"?

"Only an hour? I may have to talk fast".......and they both laughed.

LOOKING BACK

"I lived the good life, went to the best schools, dined at only the finest restaurants and socialized from time to time with the rich and famous. The first car I ever drove was a Porsche. Now it's gone, all of it; the car, the house, the land, the business and the money. I don't know how I missed all the signs. We all did. It never occurred to any of us that this beautiful woman who stood by my mother and helped raise me could have been plotting against us all these years. We were all taken in by her smile and her charms. It's all so clear to me now........... Perhaps

I should start at the beginning".

Spring of 1965

My parents met on a college campus in

upstate New York. It was a moment that neither

of them ever forgot. Winter was finally over. The

sun was shining for the first time in months.

There wasn't a cloud in the sky and the birds

seemed to be chirping a love song. The fragrance

of newly cut grass filled the air and the flowers

were in bloom in an array of vivid color. It was 2

pm and as he hurried across the courtyard to teach

his last class of the day, he saw her. The balmy

breeze had swept her long light blond hair back,

accentuating her facial features. He could see the

light reflecting in her crystal blue eyes. As she turned, their eyes met. Her smile sent a wave of warmth that permeated every cell of his body. As he approached, he said "Hello, I'm Marcus, Marcus Donnelly".

"Juliette Lang, nice to meet you".

She reached out to shake his hand and as their hands touched, they both felt a spark. It was love at first sight. She was mesmerized by his charm and incredibly good looks. He was a few inches away from her, yet she could smell a hint of musk in his cologne. Musk is one of those scents that makes her weak in the knees. For a moment she was taking him all in. He's tall, she thought, just a little taller than me about 6 feet. She could see the outline of his muscular frame through his tailored burgundy shirt. He seemed to have a tan and his wavy chocolate brown hair was styled in a way that brought out the green in his hazel green eyes.

Can it be that this man is interested in me? She thought. God, I hope he's single. A moment later he said, "I need to get to class. Are you free this afternoon, perhaps we can meet for coffee"? The gentleness of his voice melted her like snow on a sunny day.

"I'd like that", she said. And so, they met at 4:30 that afternoon. It was your typical first date but as they learned a little more about each other, they were amazed to see how much they had in common. She was 25 with a bachelor's degree in accounting. She enrolled as a student at the Community College to learn about hotel management and to hone her culinary skills.

Marcus was 31 and a professor of business
administration at the College. They were both
raised in the northeast. Juliette was an only child
and Marcus had one sister. Their favorite season
was winter with the crisp cold weather and the
beauty that comes with each snow fall. On both
of their list of musts, they desired to one day live
in New England and own a bed and breakfast.
They were so taken by one another that time got
away from them.

      "Is it seven already? Juliette was
checking the time. I need to get home; I have a
paper due tomorrow that needs a few last-minute
changes". He didn't want the night to end so
quickly but he didn't want to appear pushy, after
all, they just met.

      "I totally understand, he said. Are you free

on Saturday? I know this great restaurant, a quaint

place. It's in the country but not too far".

"It's a date", she said with a smile". As

they walked back to the campus, he reached for

her hand. They walked and talked and laughed.

Neither could recall a more beautiful night.

"Here we are, he said, as they approached

the parking lot, I've had such a nice time. Thank

you for agreeing to meet me for coffee". He gave

her the lightest kiss on the cheek and helped her

into her car. "I'll pick you up at 4 this Saturday".

"Where are we going"?

"To one of the quaintest vineyards in the

area". He smiled, tapped the car, as if to say

you're off, and waved goodbye.

That evening as Juliette was putting the

finishing touches on her paper, she gazed into the

night sky, closed her eyes and breathed deeply, feeling alive, happy and serene, re-living each moment.

The week dragged on and on. It seemed like an eternity until Saturday. Finally, the day arrived, and it was 4pm. The doorbell rang and her heart leapt with excitement. As she opened the door, she could smell his enticing cologne, a fragrance she would always associate with him. She leaned forward to give him a typical hello hug, one she gives to all of her friends, but to her surprise she was in his arms embracing him. She looked up and as their eyes met, he kissed her softly and gently. "I can get used to this kind of hello" he said with a huge grin, and they both laughed. "Are you ready", he asked?

"I sure am", she said; and they made their way to his car. It was a short ride to the winery.

" Ventosa Vineyards? she said, reading the sign to the entrance of the vineyard. I've never heard of this place".

"Really? It's been here for quite a long time. Do you drink wine?", he asked.

"Occasionally, but I have never found one that I really like".

"The wines they make here are quite different so you may find that one special wine you have been looking for. I made arrangements for us to take the wine tour before dinner".

"Sounds good to me", she said with a smile.

Ventosa Vineyards was one of the finest vineyards in the area. It was quaint and rustic all at the same time. Both the terrace & the cafe overlooked the vineyard & Seneca Lake. The view was breathtaking. Marcus opened the door and motioned a gentleman's hand allowing her to step inside first.

"Mr. Donnelly, how are you this evening"?

"Wonderful Sal, just wonderful. he said, unable to hide his excitement. This is Juliette".

" How do you do Miss"? Out of the corner of her eye she caught a nod of approval. "I see you have arranged for a tour before dinner, right this way".

The tour amazed Juliette. The vineyard used oak barrels and huge stainless-steel silos that held the fermenting grape juice. The bottling area was smaller than she imagined and as they looked out over the vineyard, she

understood the charm that Marcus was referring
to. It was as if they had been transported to
Tuscany. It was impressive, educational and
romantic all at the same time and she was so glad
they were here.

There were so many varieties of wine,
whites, reds, blushes, dry, sweet and dessert
wines. Many varieties were familiar to her, like,
Pinot Noir, Riesling and Chardonnay. Then there
were others that were unfamiliar such as,
Lemberger, Vino Rosso, and her favorite,
Sangiovese.

They spent the better part of an hour
tasting all of them. Marcus was amazed at her
ability to pick up the subtleness of the different
wines including the strawberry notes in the
Sangiovese. "I'm feeling a little tipsy she said

holding onto his arm. Perhaps it's time for dinner".

They were seated on the second story balcony overlooking the vineyard and Lake Seneca. Each time the cafe door opened; a smell reminiscent of Italy filled the air. There was a light breeze and the sun was just starting to set. "This place is lovely" said Juliette.

"I'm glad you like it. I have been coming here since I was a child. It was one of my parent's favorite places".

Marcus ordered a sampling of several menu items. They started with warm Brie topped with a reduction of raspberry coulis and served with toasted baguette slices. Then came the grilled chicken salad followed by the vineyards signature Garlic Artisan pizza with escarole sautéed in extra virgin olive oil, garlic, Marsala wine, Salami, Capicola, Prosciutto and cheese. Everything was delicious. They talked and ate and talked some more. Things couldn't be more perfect.

As the sun was setting, a four-piece band began playing music at the far end of the balcony. After dinner they danced under the stars. It was a magical evening. Just before leaving, Marcus leaned forward and said,

"I really like you Juliette and I want to see much more of you". Her heart felt like it would leap out of her chest but before she could say anything, he continued...... "unfortunately the college has a strict policy prohibiting professors from dating their students. You are not my student, but you are a student at the college. I think it would be best if we only saw one another occasionally and met away from the area of the college". Her heart sank with disappointment, but she knew he was right. Regaining her composure, she said,

"that's fine...and by the way, she smiled brightly, I like you too". And so, it was decided, they would hide their relationship until graduation.

It was a year of secrets, adventure and fun. There was a thrilling danger that ignited their desire for one another. One of their favorite rendezvous locations was the vineyard where they had their first date. It was close by yet off the beaten path. Each weekend they planned chance meetings at a different location. Sometimes they went to the beach where they would swim, jump waves and of course casually fall into one another. It was thrilling and sensual. Their meetings in the city had to be less obvious. They would meet at different locations like the observation deck of the Empire State building. Sometimes they would meet for lunch at the famous Katz Diner. Other times they met for dinner at Sardi's, in the theatre district. Every date was skillfully planned and always appeared to be a chance meeting.

There was the time they each bought a ticket to a Broadway play and arrived separately. Of course, their seats were together. Once seated they began their typical introductions. Hi, I'm Marcus, do you come to the theatre often? After a few weeks they decided to really play up the chance meeting by pretending to be someone else. On August 10th they met at

the New York State Theatre in Lincoln Center to

see the opening production of Carousel. As they

introduced themselves, Juliette told Marcus she

was Sandra, an airline stewardess. They began a

steamy conversation and started to act out the roll

of a flirtatious stewardess and an interested pilot.

The conversation was intensely stimulating, so

much so that once the lights dimmed, Marcus

quietly reach over and ran his masculine hand up

her thigh. She shivered as it took her breath

away. They both appeared to be strangers

engrossed in the play, but more often than not,

they were engrossed in each other.

One Saturday afternoon in December

they accidentally ran into each other while

Christmas shopping. Juliette was with two of her

closest friends, Melissa, a pudgy average looking girl with mousy brown hair, brown eyes and an unmistakable beauty mark over her left lip, which made her self-conscious, and Angelica, a petite red head beauty. Melissa was Juliette's oldest and dearest friend. They had been inseparable since grade school. Both Melissa and Angelica were trying on dresses. Melissa needed something more casual and Juliette had just grabbed something off the rack for her.

As she turned quickly to head back to the dressing room, she walked right into Marcus, who was admiring a glass ornament. The ornament flew out of his hand crashing to the floor. "I'm so sorry she said as she lifted her head and looked directly at him.

" MARCUS"!!! She exclaimed. "Are you

alright?"

"I'm fine, he said but I can't say the same for that ornament", pointing to the pile of broken glass on the floor. They both laughed as their eyes locked with an excitement visible to those around them. Hearing the crash, Melissa peered out of the dressing room and observed the interaction between Juliette and Marcus. She was puzzled for the moment because she had known Juliette since they were children and Juliette did not mention an attraction to anyone. Come to think of it, Juliette had been extra happy recently, almost giddy. She often bailed on weekend plans saying she had to study. Hmmmm, Melissa wondered, could it be that Juliette is in a relationship? It can't be.... she would have told me. Wouldn't she?

"Are you here alone?" Marcus asked.

"No, I'm here with two of my friends. I'd better go before they wonder what is going on and start putting the pieces together."

"I really don't want you to go yet. I have an idea, he pointed to the broken glass on the floor. That ornament was a gift for a coworker, she's about your age. We have a gift exchange tomorrow at work, so I need to find something else. Can you stay a moment longer and help a stranger pick out a new gift? After all, he said in a flirtatious manner, it is your fault that I broke the ornament."

"OK, but quickly." She looked around carefully.

There on a mannequin was a beautiful pashmina scarf. It was cream with splashes of bright colors. The perfect complement to any attire.   After handing him the scarf she said,

"I think your co-worker will like this. I really need to go."   And she hurried back to the dressing room. Her face was flushed.

"Juliette, Melissa said, who is that"?

"What do you mean, who is who"?

"Mr. Tall dark and handsome .... I saw how you were looking at him."

"Don't be silly, said Juliette, I was just flustered because I ran right into the guy."

"From the look on his face Juliette, he is definitely interested in you. Did you at least get his name"?

"No, I didn't think to ask."

"Well what were you doing all that time"?

She wished Melissa would stop the third degree.

"I was helping him find a gift for a co-worker because, thanks to me, he broke the gift he just picked out." She felt bad about lying. After all, they had been friends for as long as Juliette could remember, and they never kept secrets. One day soon I will be able to tell her, thought Juliette, but for now, I cannot risk anyone knowing.

That night her mind kept wandering to the accidental meeting. She breathed a long deep breath and closed her eyes as she recalled how it felt falling into his arms. There was a thrill that she couldn't explain, a secret that only she and Marcus shared. That chance meeting lit a fire inside her, she desired him like never before.

Juliette was not the only one recalling their chance meeting. Melissa ran the scene over and over again in her mind. She knew Juliette was hiding something from her and she was determined to find out what.

In the wee hours of Christmas morning Marcus called Juliette. "Hi beautiful he said, Merry Christmas."

" Beautiful? she relied with a question...it's 5am, I probably look a sight. Why are you calling so early?" she asked.

"Because I just left a gift for you on your front porch. Hurry and go get it before someone notices."

"A gift for me? That is so sweet, hold on I'll be right back." As she opened the door, he came from around the building and hurried in.

"Oh my gosh, she said hugging him. Merry Christmas! I can't believe you're here."

He kissed her passionately then said,

" I really wanted us to spend some time together this morning, but it has to be brief." He handed her the wrapped box he was carrying. "Here is your present", he said with a smile. Inside was a beautiful cream scarf, large enough to wrap around her shoulders on cool nights. It was the very one she had chosen for him in the store.

"I thought this was for a co-worker."

"It was but I saw how much you liked it, so I bought it especially for you. When we are apart, you can wrap it around yourself to keep warm and think of me. It will be like I'm here with you."

"Awww, that is so sweet", she said as she

hugged and then kissed him. "Okay, I have something for you too." From under the tree, she retrieved a beautifully wrapped box. "Merry Christmas Marcus." Inside was an elegant day planner for the following year and a Monte Blanc pen.

He was touched by her thoughtfulness.

"I love them, thank you", he said. "I should really leave, but I would like us to have our own Christmas dinner tomorrow. Are you free"?

"Let me think, she said with a pensive look....hmmmm, for you? I'll make the time." And they both laughed.

"Great, I'll meet you in the city, at our rendezvous spot, at 7." He gave her a long passionate kiss and slipped out before anyone could see him.

That afternoon, Juliette spent time with her parents. Between classes, papers, friends and of course her time with Marcus, she hadn't seen her family in months.

"So, what is going on in your life? Asked her mother, how's school? Are you seeing anyone"?

"No, I'm not seeing anyone. I don't have time. I'm really busy with my classes and assignments. Life is good though...Hey, I learned to make creme brûlé last week, which came out perfect...if I do say so myself", she said with a smile. Great, she thought, now I'm lying to my family.

"Creme brûlé? Asked her father. Where's

mine"? He had the sweet tooth in the family.

"I'll make you some the next time I visit, promise." She had a special place in her heart for her dad. Being the only child, and a girl, he treated her like a princess.

"So mom, dad, how's everything with you"? .... and the small talk continued.

"Do you know yet what day graduation will be"? Asked her father.

"Not yet, but it is usually early May....and I can't wait". Well, at least she wasn't lying about that.

"There's something different about you Jules, said her father, I can't quite put my finger on it."

"I noticed that too, her mom chimed in, you have a spark about you."

"Well maybe I just like my classes. After all, I'm following my passion."

Juliette loved her family and really enjoyed sharing the holidays with them but this time she couldn't wait to leave. Between the inquisition, dinner and gifts she wouldn't have time to stop by Melissa's. This would be the first time in her life that she didn't spend some time with her best friend on Christmas. Before she left her parent's, she gave a quick call to Melissa. "I'm so sorry, she said, but I got detained at my parents and it's late."

"It's Christmas Juliette, said Melissa. We always spend time together on Christmas".

"I know, but I just can't make it today.".

"What about tomorrow night"?

" I can't tomorrow. I have so much to do

before my classes start again next week. Maybe later in the week."

"I'll be out of town later in the week."

"I'll call you next week and we'll get together, I promise."

Melissa couldn't believe it. She knew Juliette was lying. Whatever or whoever it is, has taken my place.

The following night at 7pm, Marcus and Juliette met in the city. Each took their own subway in and met at 5th Ave and 53rd St, nearest to the restaurant. It was a cold breezy evening and the air had that unique smell of an impending snowfall. As Juliette emerged from the subway, she spotted Marcus. Their eyes met and they embraced.

"I hope you haven't been waiting too long,

it's freezing." said Juliette.

"Not at all, I just got here. The restaurant is only a few short blacks away. Shall we"? Marcus said as he took her arm. The walk was exhilarating. They arrived a few minutes later. "Club 21, here we are", said Marcus. They walked in and the place was magnificent. "Let me check your coat." Said Marcus. As he helped her off with her coat, he was mesmerized by her beauty. She was wearing an Emerald green dress that was fitted at the waist with a broad band. The top of the dress was covered in lace and appliques, it had lace cap sleeves and a lace back that ended in a "V" just above the waste-band. The bottom of the dress had large relaxed pleats that accentuated her curves. She wore 2" spike heels that accentuated her tight bottom and lengthened her sultry legs.

Marcus could feel his body tingling with excitement as he gazed upon her beauty.

"WOW! said Marcus. You look absolutely beautiful"! Juliette blushed and with a flirtatious grin she said,

"I wore this just for you". He could feel his excitement increasing. Surely, she was the sexiest woman in the room. I am one lucky guy, he thought. They were taken to the second-floor dining room and seated in a semi-circular booth. The tables were elegantly set with fine linens, china and crystal. In the center of the table were 3 small candles which gave the table a warm glow. Since neither of them had been here before, the waiter offered some history about the restaurant, suggested a tour of the wine cellar and informed them that dinner came as a 4course meal, the appetizer, mid-course, main-course and dessert. It was difficult to choose, as all of the menu items were tempting.

Juliette started with Crab Cake with apple, celery and fennel macédoine. Marcus ordered the Octopus Carpaccio with citrus, basil oil, Kalamata olives and a za'atar vinaigrette. Each item was masterfully plated and equally delicious. Between courses, they talked, laughed, flirted and savored every moment together. As they were about to kiss the waiter appeared with the mid-course. They both blushed, thanked the waiter and then quietly chuckled. Juliette took a bite of her ricotta cheese Agnolotti with truffle cream. She had heard about truffles but never had them. To her surprise, the taste was light and delightful. Marcus chose Lobster ravioli with lump crab meat, trout roe, tarragon and a lobster emulsion.

"You have to try this" he said as he put a fork full on her bread plate.

"I'm not a lobster lover, but this is amazing". Time seemed to fly by. It was 8:30 when the main course arrived. They decided to share the main courses which consisted of Dover sole with asparagus and lemon beurre blanc and Rhan Duck a L'Orange with caramelized endives and maple-mace jus. Each was a masterpiece and they couldn't imagine having room for dessert, so they decided to have a tour of the wine cellar first. As they passed the first-floor dining area, they saw a few celebrities. The waiter told them that the celebrities always take the same table each time they dine there. Frank Sinatra was there with his family at table 14. They saw Helen Hayes at table 2 and there at table 21, was the one and only Jackie Gleason. Does it get any better than this? They thought.

They made their way to the wine cellar and were shocked at the enormity of it all. The wine steward told them that during the Prohibition Era, the wine cellar had been designed to be invisible and was hidden from view behind a two-tone door which was built to match the brick foundation. The wine cellar was located next door in the cellar of number 19. He said that during prohibition, when the police asked the bar tenders if they kept liquor on the premises, they could honestly say no. During that time, the hidden wine cellar was the best-kept secret in

New York.

After the tour, they were escorted back to their table for dessert. There was Baked Alaska with Meyer lemon semifreddo and Cointreau as well as a delicious Saint-Domingue Chocolate Souffle with bourbon caramel anglaise and smoked vanilla ice cream. Neither could have imagined a more perfect Christmas dinner.

After dinner they took a horse and buggy ride to Rockefeller Center to see the Christmas tree. As the evening progressed a light snow fall began. It was beautiful to watch the snow fall streaming down in front of the streetlights. They held hands, walked, talked and kissed under the moon lit snow.

Because it was late and there so few people out and about, they rode the same train home. Marcus wanted to make certain Juliette arrived home safely. The snow was coming down much harder now and mounting up quickly. They found a secluded area about a block from her apartment and kissed good night.

"I'll call you tomorrow", he said, and he watched her until she was safely inside.

Juliette was happier than she had ever been but couldn't help feeling bad about missing Christmas with Melissa. Between school and her time with Marcus, she had no real time for her friends or family. Fortunately, Angelica was easy going and never got upset if Juliette could not spend time with her. Melissa on the other hand, sulked. The following Monday Juliette called Melissa, but there was no answer, that was at 1pm. At 4:30 Juliette had called again. NO answer! Just great, she thought. She called every few days over the course of three weeks, then out of desperation she sent a note that said: *Hi Melissa it's Juliette. I have been trying to reach you, but you are never home. How about getting together for dinner on Monday night? Give me a call*, but Melissa never did not respond.

The winter months were hard. Traveling any distance was near impossible. The never-ending snowstorms kept their secret meetings to a minimum. However, this gave her a little more time for her friends. On a Saturday in late January she made arrangements to meet Angelica for lunch and asked Angelica to invite Melissa. Angelica was happy to get together with Juliette. She missed seeing her but was not the type to be jealous or petty. They exchanged late

Christmas gifts and seldom spoke. As they sat down for lunch, they talked about the day to day goings on. Juliette was so concerned about Melissa's absence that it took her 45 minutes to notice the ring on Angelica's hand.

"OH MY GOSH, your engaged!!!! They were squealing with excitement. Let mc see your ring. It is so beautiful. I'm so happy for you Angie. When is the big day"?

"Genaro and I haven't decided yet. He proposed on Christmas. I've been waiting until I could tell you in person."

"Does Melissa know"? Asked Juliette.

"Yes, but she has been acting really weird lately. She never wants to get together and gets really annoyed if I mention you. Did the two of you have a fight"?

"No, but she won't answer my calls. It's very strange. She has been upset ever since Christmas."

"I have an idea, said Angelica. Melissa's' birthday is in two weeks. Let's give her a party at my house."

"That's a great idea, said Juliette. "I'll bake her favorite cake and bring some champagne." Checking their calendars, they decided on February 7th.

The party went off without a hitch. Melissa was so excited to be the center of attention that she temporarily forgot why she was mad at Juliette. They talked like nothing ever happened. Juliette's cake was a huge hit with everyone, but especially with Melissa because it made her feel special and important to Juliette.

As the party came to a close, all of the guests had gone leaving just the three close friends.

"I have a great idea, said Melissa. Why don't the three of us have dinner together next Saturday"?

"Sorry Melissa but Genaro and I have plans that night...it's Valentine's Day, remember"?

"Hmmm, I forgot. Well how about you Juliette? You're not seeing anyone, are you"?

Oh no, thought Juliette...here we go again, one lie after another.

"Sorry Melissa but I promised my parents I would spend time with them."

"Your parents"?

"Yeah, I know it seems odd, but I have been so busy with school that I haven't had much time for them or anything else. I'll give you a call later this week and we can plan something, OK"?

"Sure." Melissa felt as if her balloon just deflated.

Marcus and Juliette agreed to take a chance and have a romantic dinner at home on Valentine's Day. After weeks of barely seeing one another, Marcus wanted everything to be perfect. He planned the evening down to the tiniest detail and prepared a special dinner. Juliette arrived at his home precisely at 7:30. She was hoping that most people would be in their homes by that time but took no chances. She wore a dark blue business suit accented with the scarf Marcus gave her for Christmas and wore her hair up. Although she had no need for glasses, she purchased a pair just for this occasion. In her right hand she carried a briefcase, giving the impression that she was there on business.

Marcus did a double take. Fighting back laughter, he shook her hand and then invited her in. Once they were behind closed doors, he kissed her.

"Well well, he said looking her over. No-one would ever know the real reason you are here", he said chiding her. He grabbed her tight and kissed her with more passion than ever before.

"I could get used to this he said. You should keep this outfit for a later time." He had one eyebrow raised in a sexy flirtatious look. She understood exactly what he meant, which sent chills up her spine. Her body was tingling with anticipation of the day they would be together.

"Dinner is ready", he said as he escorted her to the table and pulled out her chair.

She was amazed at all the trouble he went to, the table was set with fine linens, china, Waterford crystal and a crystal candle holder that held one lit candle. There was soft music playing in the background and the wonderful aroma coming from the kitchen was almost intoxicating. He poured the wine and raised his glass,

"A toast to the most beautiful girl in the world." They clanged glasses and took a sip.

"My favorite, she said, you remembered.".

"Of course, I remembered. Happy Valentine's Day Juliette." He pulled out a small box from his coat pocket and handed it to her. Inside was a gold necklace with a charm in the shape of a key. The card read; you hold the key

to my heart. She was overjoyed,

"Oh Marcus, thank you", she said as she

jumped into his arms and kissed him. Dinner

lasted about an hour followed by slow dancing

and kissing. It was the best Valentine's Day

Juliette ever had.

The following weekend they met in

the city and the week after they met at the

vineyard. Between school and her time with

Marcus, Juliette had no time for anyone else.

Melissa had called each week suggesting a time to

get together but Juliette always had a reason why

she could not meet. Melissa's anger burned

within her.

March and April flew by and now It was

just three weeks until graduation, Juliette

wondered if she could wait another three weeks to be with Marcus as the desire to be with him flooded her mind. She thought of him day and night imagining his strong hands caressing her body. His thoughts and desires mimicked hers. The waiting and wanting were consuming them.

Melissa made one more call to arrange a time together.

"Sorry Melissa, I am swamped right now. I'll see you Saturday at the graduation and at my place after. How about getting together on Monday? I have time off before I start working. We can meet for lunch and catch up." Melissa wanted to say no but she also wanted to spend time alone with Juliette, so she reluctantly agreed to meet her at 1pm on Monday, just two days after graduation.

THE SECRET'S OUT

Finally, the day of graduation came. The graduation was held outdoors. Rows upon rows of white chairs lined the courtyard with family and friends. The graduates were seated on a stage that was set up for this special occasion. As the valedictorian gave her speech, Juliette 's mind was focused on the beauty of her surroundings. The grass was green, flowers were in bloom, the sun was shining, and her hair was gently blowing in the wind. This reminded her of an earlier time. It reminded her of the day she met Marcus. She was reliving their entire year when she noticed the first row of students rising to form a line and receive their diploma's. Soon it was her turn.

"Juliette Lang". As she walked across the stage, she could hear applause. She glanced over the crowd and saw her parents, Melissa, Angelica and Genaro. Marcus was on stage with the other faculty members. As Juliette passed him, he gave her smile and a thumbs up.

The ceremony ended with the traditional tossing of the caps then Juliette went into the crowd to greet her parents and friends.

"We are so proud of you honey", said her mother. Her father gave her a big hug. "So, now that you have graduated, when can I expect the creme brûlé you have been promising me"?

"Well, sooner than you think dad. I just happened to have made it for the party." Melissa, Angelica and Genaro each congratulated Juliette. They were happy for her and happy that her life would again have room for them. As Juliette was saying,

"Come on everyone, let's go back to my place", Marcus approached to congratulate her. He was so proud of her and so happy that they would no longer have to hide their relationship. Since she was surrounded by her family and friends, he had to be patient a little longer.

"Everyone, this is Dr. Marcus Donnelly, he is a professor in the finance department. Professor Donnelly, this is my mother and father,

Mr. & Mrs. Lang."

"It's very nice to meet you Mr.& Mrs. Lang, you must be so proud", he said as he shook their hands.

"And these are a few of my friends, Angelica, Genaro, and Melissa." While shaking hands, they each commented in turn,

"nice to meet you." Melissa knew that she had seen this man before but couldn't place him.

"Professor Donnelly, we are going back to my place for an informal celebration, nothing fancy. Some of the other graduates and faculty will be there. Would you like to join us? she asked as she scribbled something on a piece of paper. Here's my address." She handed him a folded piece of paper. As he glanced at it, he had to contain himself. The paper read...Finally!!!!! I can't wait for tonight! His heart was beating fast and he could feel the excitement traveling throughout his body.

"I think I can make it." he said, with as pensive a look as he could muster.

"Great" she said, with the beautiful smile that always melts him. See you later".... And he was off.

Marcus arrived at 7:30. The party was in full swing. People were talking, laughing and dancing to the loud music. There was a small buffet. The beverage selection included her favorite wine, the one she found at Ventosa Vineyards last year. Melissa was staring at Marcus trying to place him. As the evening progressed, Juliette and Marcus were intently talking and the expression on both their faces gave Melissa a sense of Deja vu. Suddenly Melissa remembered. This is the guy who Juliette ran into when we were Christmas shopping. So, she was in a relationship with him. How long has this been going on, she wondered and why has she been keeping it secret? Melissa felt both intrigued and betrayed. Juliette purposefully lied to her. Melissa's blood began to boil. She left abruptly without a single good-bye. All the way home all she could think about was that he is the reason that Juliette doesn't have time for me anymore.

When the last guests were about to leave Marcus said,

"why don't I help you clean up before I leave". The other guests offered as well but she insisted that there wasn't enough clean-up for more than two people.

They were finally alone.

"Well then... since you are no longer a student, I would like to officially ask if you would like to be my girlfriend."

"Hmmmm, let me think about It, she teased, then she laughed and said, "what do you think"? She pulled him toward her and kissed him. He didn't know if he could wait much longer.

"Why don't you slip into something more comfortable Juliette...I'll tidy up here." She nodded and left to ready herself for a night of long-awaited passion. Marcus quickly tidied up the apartment and removed his shirt and tie. He put on just a dab of the cologne she liked so much and tapped on her bedroom door.

"May I come in", he asked? She opened the door to see the most magnificent man standing in front of her, manly and ready to take her. She was exquisite, wearing a semi see through pale pink nightgown. He could see every detail of her body. The time was finally here. This was their moment.

"I love you Juliette". He took her into his arms and the passion began. He held her and kissed her, working his way down her body. Her skin felt like the finest silk and was softer than a cloud. They made love tenderly, then passionately then tenderly again. They were in perfect harmony, like a choreographed dance.

In the morning he handed her with a small envelope. Inside was a note that read... Now that school is over, how about a relaxing get away?

Juliette looked puzzled.

"Away? Where"?

"Have you ever been to the Bahamas"?

"No, but I've heard that it is beautiful."

"OK, it's settled. We leave tomorrow."

"Tomorrow? She squealed with excitement. You had this all planned, didn't you"?

"It's my gift to you. I wanted to give you something special and what better time is there? You don't start your new job for 2 weeks."

"Oh my gosh there is so much I have to do. You are amazing, she said. I need to get going."

"OK, I'll get out of your way and I'll be here to pick you up at 9am." They kissed once more before he left.

The day flew by quickly. True to his

word, Marcus arrived at precisely 9am. Juliette was dressed in pale peach Bermuda shorts with a peach and white stripped sleeveless blouse, white sandals and a peach and white hat which was perfect for the beach.

"Wow, look at you. I don't know if I can resist you long enough for us to make it to the beach. He gave her a long kiss then said, we need to get to the airport."

The flight left and arrived on time. Once they were on the island, they checked into their beach front cottage and fell into each other's arms. There was no restraint. The passion that united them was greater than either of them ever imagined.

Monday 1pm

Melissa was excited to be at Juliette's

apartment. She had a great time at the graduation party and thought about all of the wonderful times she and Juliette spent together. In fact, thinking about it made her feel silly for being upset at all. Juliette is a good friend and she has been busy with school and work. I need to be more understanding. She rang the bell, no answer. That's odd, she rang it again then checked the time. 1:05. She rang the bell several more times but there was no answer. Juliette wasn't home. Are you kidding me? She thought. Here I trusted you. How could you do this ? It's him, isn't it? It's him!!!!!! The more she thought about it, the angrier she got. She went home and dialed Juliette's number. Ring, ring, ring, ring, no answer there either. By the 10th ring, she hung up and started ranting to herself; He is the reason for all of this. He has taken you away from me. I

thought you were my friend. One day I'll get even.

I'll get even with them both!

LOVE BLOOMS

The week in the Bahamas was magical. When they weren't making love, they swam in the warm clear water at Harbour Island. Harbour Island is a beach with a 3 mile long stretch of soft pink sand which makes it one of the most unusual beaches in the world. By day they snorkeled and by night they walked along the sandy beach hand in hand. One afternoon, they took a tour of the island and bought a few souvenirs.

"I think Melissa would like this hat." As she said it, she remembered her date with Melissa. "Oh no"! She exclaimed.

"What is it Juliette, what's wrong"?

"I made a date with Melissa for the day we left and with all of the excitement, I forgot to cancel. Oh my gosh. She must be really upset. She has been distant for some time and we were finally getting back to the way things used to be between us."

"She'll understand, Marcus said with a reassuring gesture."

"I don't know Marcus. She has been acting weird for months now."

"Well when we get back, you can explain everything to her. You said she is your oldest and closest friend so I'm sure once you explain, she will understand." "I certainly hope so." She said.

"You can't do anything about it right now, so put it out of your mind and enjoy the time we have together."

"You're right Marcus, I'll call her and straighten this all out when we return. No sense ruining out trip."

A few days later they arrived home. There were 12 missed calls from Melissa and one harsh message... *"Thanks for standing me up. I guess you're with HIM now. So much for friendship."* Slam. Juliette looked horrified.

"What is it"? asked Marcus

"It's Melissa, she is beyond mad. I'll call her later."

Once the unpacking was done, it was time

to make the dreaded call. She couldn't decide

which she wanted more, to have Melissa answer

the phone or for the call to go to voice mail. Two

rings...three…four

"Hello Juliette"! Her tone was harsh.

"Hi Melissa. I got your messages; I am so

sorry. Can we meet for coffee tonight? I would

like to explain everything to you." Melissa was

sure she would never agree to see Juliette again

but the thought of knowing EVERYTHING was

something she couldn't resist.

"Fine what time would you like me to

come over"?

"How about meeting me at the diner on

Main St., we can talk over pie...like we always do

when we have something important to talk about."

"I'll meet you at 7", said Melissa. Then the

phone went dead. Well, that went better than I expected, thought Juliette.

Juliette arrived a few minutes early and took a seat in their favorite booth. She thought about all the times they would sit in this booth, sometimes for hours, talking about school, boyfriends, parents and their future dreams. Melissa had yearned for a boyfriend. Yet even at age 24 there was no boyfriend in sight. This is going to be hard, thought Juliette. I really hope she understands. She looked up just as Melissa was entering the diner. She waved her over to the booth.

"Our special booth, Juliette said with a smile. I was so glad that no-one was sitting here when I arrived." Melissa shrugged as if to say, who cares, then she sat down. They placed their orders then Melissa said sharply,

"so, what's going on Juliette"? Then she waited, an angry look washed over her face.

"I have been seeing Marcus Donnelly for over a year. I'm sorry but I couldn't tell you, she said quickly. The school has a strict policy about professors dating their students and even though he was not my professor, he is a professor there and I was a student. We couldn't risk getting caught."

"I don't understand, said Melissa, we have always told each other everything. I was never at that school and I don't know anyone there so who could I tell"? There was silence. "What are you saying, you couldn't trust me? Did I tell anyone about the time you smoked a cigarette when we were in Jr. High? No! So, what gives? Who are you? You are certainly not acting like a friend...and by the way, I remember seeing Marcus last Christmas when we were shopping. I asked you about him and you lied right to my face." The ranting went on and on. No matter what Juliette said or how much she tried to explain, Melissa continued to rant.

Finally, Juliette said,

"Melissa, we have been friends forever and yes, in hindsight I should have told you, but I can't go back. Please forgive me."

"I don't know, said Melissa. It really doesn't matter anymore because I am moving to California next week."

"California? Why"?

"I haven't made much of myself here, I am not seeing anyone and the weather in California is great all year. Besides, I need a change, a fresh start."

"I can't believe it, I'll miss you."

"Why would you miss me? It's not like we see each other anymore." Juliette couldn't help but feel ashamed of the way she had treated her friend.

"I'm sorry Melissa, really and I will miss you very much." They got up to leave. It was nearly 10 O'clock. "Please keep in touch, said Juliette. I want to know all about it." Juliette started to hug Melissa, but Melissa did not respond in kind. Well, at least she didn't pull away, thought Juliette. They left and the two went their separate ways. Juliette was sad to think that her lifelong friend was unwilling to understand but with Melissa moving away, there was little she could do about it.

A week later, Juliette started her new job, as a sous chef at a nearby restaurant. She was so excited to be cooking at a real restaurant with paying customers. The job was demanding. She worked 6 days a week until 1am. This left little time for her and Marcus to get together. They made the most of their time together by pre-planning everything. Weeks turned into months and before they knew it the holidays were here. Thankfully the restaurant was closed on Christmas, New Year's Eve and New Year's Day.

Christmas was a special time for Juliette and her family. This year was even more special because there was no more hiding their relationship which allowed Marcus to go with Juliette to her parents' home for Christmas. Mr.

& Mrs. Lang liked Marcus. They had met him a few times and could see how much he loved their daughter. While Juliette was in the kitchen helping her mother, Marcus took a few minutes alone to speak with her father. "Mr. Lang, he began. I want you to know how much I care for your daughter, in fact, I love her. I would like to ask you for her hand in marriage."

Mr. Lang was impressed with the amount of respect shown by his soon to be son in law. "I would be honored to give you her hand in marriage and they embraced."

"Mr. Lang, one more thing, I haven't asked her yet so please don't say anything to her. If you tell Mrs. Lang, which is fine with me, please ask her not to say anything. I want the moment to be just right."

"Very well my boy, very well."

On the way home Juliette couldn't help but notice a change in Marcus. He seemed overly happy.

"What were you and my father talking about"?

"Oh, sports, you know guy things."

"Hmmmm and that is why you are so happy"?

"Well, that and the fact that I told him how much you mean to me. He seemed genuinely happy to hear it."

"Oh Marcus, you are so sweet. That's why I love you so much.

"You know, I have a little surprise waiting for you at home."

"Really, should I guess"?

"You'll see." And he did. A night of love and passion. What could be better than this? They both thought.

On New Year's Eve, they hosted a small party at Marcus's home. Marcus was in charge of the decorations while Juliette tended to the food. Marcus strung tiny white lights from the ceiling and on the balcony. He set up a long table in the living room, covered it with a red holiday tablecloth and set out the chaffing dishes for Juliette. He accented the table with small bouquets of fresh flowers and candles filled the living room and the balcony with the scent of Christmas pine. He bought special New Year's champagne flutes for each guest as well as matching plates and napkins. There were decorative hats, confetti pulls and noise makers.

He even hired a DJ.

Thank goodness his place could accommodate a party like this, she thought. Juliette was in the kitchen putting the finishing touches on her Hors d'oeuvres. There were mini crab cakes with a remoulade sauce, grilled teriyaki chicken skewers, Swedish meatballs, spinach and cheese tartlets and an array of fruits, cheeses, crackers and desserts. The guests had arrived precisely at 9pm. Each brought an expensive bottle of their liking. There were bottles of cognac, wine, port, bourbon and scotch. It was their first party together and everyone was having fun mingling, eating, drinking and dancing.

Late in the evening, Juliette and Marcus wanted to carve out a few minutes of alone time so Marcus took her by the hand and

led her outside to the balcony. The cold air felt

good after spending so much time preparing and

playing host and hostess. They were marveling

about the night and how wonderful the party had

turned out. The stars were shining against the

dark night sky, reminding Juliette of their first

date at the vineyard. Suddenly they saw flurries

of snow. There was nothing like the majestic

beauty of a snowfall under a moonlit sky. At the

stroke of midnight Marcus knelt on one knee,

professed his love and asked Juliette to marry

him. He popped open a small black felt box.

Inside was a 1 carat princess cut diamond ring

accented with channel set baguettes. The ring

was set in both platinum and rose gold. As soon

as Juliette said yes, he slipped the ring on her

finger. Every facet of the diamond sparkled under the starry sky. It was the most beautiful ring she had ever seen, and she loved it almost as much as she loved Marcus.

A few days later they flew to Miami to visit Marcus's parents. Mr. & Mrs. Donnelly had Marcus later in life, so they were up in years. They were so anxious to meet Juliette, the women who stole the heart of their son. Juliette was nervous, meeting her prospective in-laws for the first time. Mr. & Mrs. Donnelly were waiting at the airport. As soon as they caught a glimpse of Marcus, they were overjoyed and waved their arms to get is attention. Juliette couldn't help but notice the love pouring out of both of them as they hugged and kissed him hello.

"Mom, Dad, this is Juliette, my fiancée."

"Oh, it is so good to finally meet you", said Mrs. Donnelly as she hugged Juliette.

"Welcome to the family" said Mr. Donnelly as he gave her a small kiss on the cheek. The visit was filled with warmth and genuine love. They reminisced over pictures of Marcus from infancy to adulthood. His parents are so proud of him and he was so loving towards them both. Juliette was pleased that she would soon be a part of this family.

They returned home excited to start planning the wedding. Juliette was happy but she felt bad that Melissa was not around to share in her joy.

Later that evening, Juliette wrote a letter to Melissa telling her all about the proposal and asking her to be a bridesmaid. It took 3 weeks to hear back but a letter from Melissa finally came.

"Dear Juliette,

I have been busy settling in. I'm working at a marketing firm in LA. It's what I always wanted to do. The move has proved itself to be a great idea. And guess what? I met a really nice guy and we have been seeing each other. His name is Michael. He is a 3rd year surgical resident.

I can't wait for you to meet him. Have you set a date for your wedding? Of course, I will be a bridesmaid. Write as soon as you can. Got to go.

Melissa"

Juliette was so relieved. Everything was falling into place. She had the love of her life and now her best friend returned.

The following months were filled

with wedding plans. Juliette and Marcus were busy with all the details. The list of things to do seemed endless, choose a cake, find a band, design invitations, make seating arrangements...the list went on and on. They chose to be married at the church where Juliette was raised. The ceremony would be simple but elegant. The restaurant where Juliette worked had a banquet hall and the owner offered to cater the food. When Juliette wasn't at work or spending time with Marcus, she and Angelica were shopping for bridal gowns, writing out the invitations and making wedding favors. Melissa could not get away but promised to be there in time to be a part of the wedding. Juliette was exhausted. No wonder people elope, she thought.

On a beautiful spring day in 1967,

five months after their engagement, they were

married. They had an idyllic church wedding

with a small bridal party which included

Angelica, as maid of honor and Melissa and Lily

were bride's maid. The best man was Marcus's

longtime friend Jason and accompanying Melissa

was the groomsman Genaro. Lily's husband

Andrew accompanied her. Juliette wore a satin

wedding gown. The top of the gown and the long

sleeves were made of intricate lace. Her hair was

swept back in a most becoming fashion and she

wore pearl stud earrings. Her delicate crown was

encircled by a two layered veil that flowed three

quarters of the way down her back and she carried

a bouquet of white roses and baby's breath.

Angelica, Melissa and Lily wore off the shoulder,

mint green evening gowns and long white gloves.

They carried bouquets of purple callas & light green orchids. The men wore black tuxedo's and black ties. Marcus had a single white rose boutonniere that matched Juliette's bouquet and the other men wore a green orchid boutonniere.

There was so much excitement in the air, and everyone was happy to be there, including the parents of the bride and groom who were ecstatic. Everyone that is, except for one undeniably quiet person in the room, Melissa. The appetizer had arrived, and it was one of Melissa's favorite dishes, eggplant rollatini, yet Melissa didn't touch it. This course was followed by French onion soup, Greek salad and a choice of prime rib or stuffed flounder. Everything was delicious. Juliette was so involved in her special day that she hadn't noticed Melissa, but Angelica couldn't help but notice. It was during the last course that Angelica finally spoke up.

"What's with you Melissa? You're acting like you're at a funeral, not a wedding. In fact, you have been acting cold and sad for the past year and a half. Why"?

"It's nothing", said Melissa.

"This is your best friend's wedding and you say it's nothing? Why aren't you happy for her. Look at her, she's beaming and so in love. What more could anyone want"?

"I don't want to talk about it."

With that Melissa walked over to the bar to get a drink. She was frustrated and angry. Michael could not accompany her. Juliette hardly said 10 words to her since she arrived yesterday but found plenty of time to talk with Angelica.

She felt alone, discarded. Friends? You think we're friends? She thought. Her mind wouldn't stop. Things are not the same, they'll never be the same. Look at them...He took her from me, and she doesn't care about me anymore, it's all about him.

Angelica was looking at the happy couple and smiling. Melissa felt betrayed. Her thoughts were all over the place.... Angelica's another one, another betrayer, Juliette's new best friend. Well we'll see how you like it when she dumps you. Her mind was overrun with thoughts of anger, betrayal and hatred. If only she could say these things, perhaps the pain would lessen. She knew she had to do something, but what?

A NEW START

Juliette and Marcus were the happiest of
newlyweds. They were in love and saw each other
as best friends. They spent as much time as
possible together and made passionate love nearly
every night. In the fall Marcus resumed his
fulltime teaching load and Juliette continued her
work as a sous chef. They both loved their
careers. As the holidays were approaching, the

restaurant became busier and busier. Suddenly Juliette was working even longer hours and Marcus was consumed with grading papers, preparing for class and writing exams. Five months into the marriage and they were finding it difficult to spend quality time together. What was once a romantic, passionate marriage was now little more than two exhausted people frustrated and at times short tempered. They longed for each other but there was so little time. They wondered how they got to this point and how they could change it.

It was a year later, and things did not change. Juliette was promoted to chef which meant higher pay but with more responsibility and more hours. Marcus was supportive but frustrated. He loved his wife and wanted her to succeed and to be happy but neither of them seemed happy these days. One night, Juliette didn't get home until 2am. She was beyond tired and next to tears. Her emotions ran high and the littlest thing seemed to irritate her. Crying had been a rarity in the past but these days, she cried over the smallest things.

"Juliette, he said softly, you cannot go on like this, we cannot go on like this. Let's try to come up with a plan. He held her in his arms and gently wiped away her tears. We got married so that we could be together but that is not happening. I've been thinking.... Do you remember when, we first met, I told you I had a dream of opening a Bed and Breakfast? She nodded her head. You said that was also a dream of yours. Juliette nodded. Why haven't we discussed it.... talked about it, ... or even dreamed about it?

"Starting a B&B takes a lot of money", said Juliette.

"Yes, I know, said Marcus, but that shouldn't keep us from coming up with a plan. Here's what I'm thinking, I have less than 2 years before I'm fully vested at the college, then I can take retirement and receive a pension, which would provide us an income while the Bed and Breakfast gets going. Before that we can save as much as possible for the down payment. What do you think"?

"I like the idea." It was the first time she smiled in days. "You can use your knowledge of finance to run the day to day operations and I can use my culinary skills to wow our guests. But best of all, we will be together." A small tear of relief trickled down her face as they embraced and sighed a sigh of relief.

"Okay, said Marcus, it's settled. Two years until we own our very own Bed and Breakfast." Juliette felt as if a weight had been lifted off her. It was the calmest moment she could remember in the past year. They were suddenly energized with the thought of owning their own business. Their plan was sure to make their dreams come true. Marcus' arms were tightly wrapped around her. She could feel the warmth of his chest washing over her like the sun on a warm summer day. He kissed her head. She felt safe and calm. No more working until 1 or 2 am, she thought, no more being told what to cook. She would create all the menus. She smiled and drifted off to sleep.

At first the excitement of their plan gave them extra energy and tolerance for work but lately each day seemed longer than the one before it and a week felt like a month. It was a struggle, like all couples they had their ups and downs, but they never let that stop then. Fourteen months later they began looking at B&B's for sale. Some were run down and would take too much capital to update them, others were overpriced, too large or too small. When they had all but given up, they saw it, the perfect Bed and Breakfast, just enough rooms to guarantee a profit but not so big that they would have to hire additional help. It was quaint and beautifully decorated. The kitchen was large with a commercial stove and oven. As they walked around, they met several of the guests all happy, with only good things to say about their stay. Many said they had stayed there multiple times. The only thing that concerned them was the price. It was higher than their budget. When they left the B&B they stopped to get dinner and to talk things over. They went back and forth with the pros and cons. In the end they decided that this was the right decision and they made an offer.

"The closing is in 2 months, Juliette gasped. There is so much to do". They were elated and nervous. This was their dream and it was finally coming true.

With the packing, licensing, setting up utilities, turning off utilities, ending the lease on their apartment and saying their good buys, the two months passed quickly. A few days before the move, Angelica invited them over for a goodbye party. When they walked into the house their eyes opened wide with surprise. Just about everyone they knew were there, Marcus and Juliette's parents, Genaro, Jason, Lily, friends from the restaurant, faculty from the college and friends they met recently as a couple. There was food, wine, music and dancing. Everyone had a great time. It was hard to end the night knowing it would be a long time before they could even return for a visit. When Juliette had a moment alone with Angelica she asked about Melissa.

"She said she couldn't make it, but I get the impression it's something else. You know how she pouts when something is bothering her. I think she and Michael are having problems."

"That's too bad, said Juliette. I hope everything works out for them." Angelica nodded, "me too".

It was the spring of 1970, a time they would never forget. New Hampshire was beautiful this time of year. The flowers were in bloom in vibrant shades of red, orange, yellow and purple. The sky was blue with not a cloud in sight and the day had finally arrived. The day they had been dreaming of for the past 4 years. Marcus had been driving for what seemed to be an eternity.

"It's just ahead". he said. They pulled onto the tree lined street. As they pulled up to the building, they were in awe of the majesty of it all. The house sat back on a small hill with lush green grass and perfectly manicured landscaping. Even from the street they could smell fresh roses and honeysuckle.

"Talk about picture perfect, Juliette said. I can't believe it, we're really doing this, our own Bed & Breakfast". She was bursting with joy. Marcus, always the gentleman, opened the door and then quickly scooped up Juliette and carried her over the threshold. Once inside they kissed.

"Our very first home together, said Marcus and our first business, wow"! They took a deep breath and started walking through the rooms on the first floor. The house was beautiful. An eclectic, late Victorian cottage home, designed mostly in a Queen Anne style. The design was complex with asymmetrical roof lines and lavish woodwork. Verandas encircled the home and offered a variety of relaxing furnishings, from comfy overstuffed chairs, to two-seater swings and large hammocks that swayed in the breeze.

The inside of the home was just as they remembered. The foyer opened into a large sitting parlor with antique furnishings, heavy draperies and a stone fireplace. In the rear of the home was the kitchen. Juliette could not wait to use her culinary skills preparing sumptuous breakfast for the guests and wonderful dinners for her and Marcus.

"This kitchen is amazing, said Juliette, it's even more impressive than when we first saw it. Look at all of the counter space, it looks big enough to sleep on".

"Really, said Marcus. Hmmm, that gives me an idea."

"What"?

"You'll see, but not now. Let's check out the upstairs."

The six guest rooms were tastefully decorated, each with its own private bath. There were 4 rooms on the second floor and 2 on the third floor. They entered one of the second story guest room. "This room is huge, she said, even with the king size bed, there's room for a 3rd guest, and I love the rust colors, they remind me of fall" As they went from room to room, they marveled over the unique differences of each. One of the rooms was decorated in shades of lavender with a queen-sized bed and a door leading to the veranda. The next room had a blue motif. The last room was decorated in muted tones of white. It had a queen bed and a balcony overlooking the pool. On the third floor was a room was painted taupe with cream accents and had a very regal looking bed. The final room was decorated in hues of fall colored leaves. It was the only guest room with a king-sized bed.

"I can't believe this is really happening, said Juliette. This is just how I imagined it when I was a little girl."

"Me too, said Marcus. .....I mean, not as a girl"...and they laughed. As they went downstairs, Juliette asked,

"when do the first guests arrive"?

"I think in about 2 weeks".

"W e l l then, Mr. Donnelly, I suggest we christen each room." There was a tantalizing twinkle in her eye. He could feel the blood rushing to his loins. Juliette's ability to please him engulfed his thoughts. They headed straight to the kitchen. Marcus had an idea, a very hot, sexy idea. Suddenly Juliette was scooped up into

Marcus' strong arms. His lips met hers as he laid
her on the counter.

"How does it feel"? He asked.

"Rather hard".

"Is it now? He said with a seductive smirk.

Maybe I should join you up there."
He climbed up and began kissing and caressing
her body. The flame that was once there was re-
ignited. Clothing was thrown everywhere as they
ravaged one another.

With so much to do to prepare for
the first guests to arrive, the next two weeks
passed quickly. First, they had to come to a
decision on how to make their B&B uniquely
different from the others in the area. All of the
other B&B's, that they visited over the past few
months, offered one entree at breakfast along with

bagels and Danish and each afternoon between 4pm & 6pm, wine was served in the living room. They considering many options then decided to offer 3 entrees for breakfast along with homemade biscuits and freshly baked bread. Rather than the typical wine in the late afternoon, they chose to have a light afternoon tea along with a variety of aperitifs, which included Sherry, Vermouth, Campari, and Dubonnet.

The B&B came with all of the furnishings, but they still needed linens, table settings, dished and cutlery. Each day was an adventure, ordering supplies, laying out new linens, testing foods for the breakfast and the afternoon tea menu and giving distinct names to each of the guest rooms. With packages arriving daily, it felt like Christmas morning every day.

They were excited, elated, and most of all happy. At the end of each busy day, they made love, every day more passionate then the one before. The night before the first guests arrived, they lay in bed, in each other's arms, completely spent. They were happier than they had been in the past two years and completely in love with one another.

"Look at us, said Marcus. We've made love every day since we moved in, a far cry from the last two years. No more working until the wee hours of the morning, no more being apart constantly. I'm so glad we decided to pursue our dream. He kissed her gently. "I love you Mrs. Donnelly".

"I love you too Marcus, more than you can imagine."

It was 6am on June 9th. They wanted to get an early start. After a quick breakfast, Marcus put on the news to hear the latest weather report. It was going to be sunny all week with temperatures in the mid 70's. That's perfect, he thought. At 7am he opened the living room windows, checked each room to see that everything was neatly organized, dusted and vacuumed. Juliette tidied up from breakfast and began making mini blueberry scones and finger sandwiches for their afternoon tea. At 9am, the florist arrived. There were two dozen pink roses arranged with baby's breath (which were ordered by Mr. Boyd as a surprise for his wife) and brightly colored arrangements of spring flowers for the living room and dining room. Juliette set each arrangement in crystal vases. She took the roses up to the Tiffany room on the second floor and placed them on an antique hope chest at the foot of the bed. The roses brightened the room. Looking around the room, Juliette felt a sense of pride. The house looked and smelled wonderful.

The first guests arrived at 10:30 and before long, they were filled to capacity. Days passed quickly and they couldn't be happier. Both were living their dream and the best part was that they were together and had time for one another, time for friends and time for family.

Several months passed and Juliette was feeling run down and tired. Marcus was concerned and suggested a visit to the doctor. She waited a few more weeks, hoping it would pass but it didn't. Marcus went with her to hear what the doctor had to say.

Dr. Stevens was thorough, full exam, blood work. Jonathan was worried. After the exam, they were led to Dr. Stevens office to discuss the findings.

"Please sit.", he said as he motioned to the chairs in front of his desk.

"Is it serious Dr"? Asked Marcus.

"No, not at all.", he chuckled.

"Then why am I so tired"? asked Juliette.

"You're pregnant, congratulations"!

"Pregnant"! They both exclaimed, eyes widening.

"I'm pregnant Marcus. We're going to have a baby."

"Oh my gosh, said Marcus. Thank you Dr. Thank you."

"I'm going to refer you to Dr. Davis. He is

an obstetrician. You can pick up his information when you check out at the front desk. Congratulations again." and he left. Marcus pulled Juliette to him and kissed her softly.

"A baby", he whispered, and they kissed again.

Life couldn't get any better. Their family and friends were happy for them. Everyone knew but Melissa. Juliette had not heard from Melissa since the wedding. She had sent a few letters but there was never a response. She decided to try one last time. Surely Melissa could not ignore this letter. Juliette kept hoping, but as the weeks passed, she had to come to the realization that their friendship was over. Just as she was about to give up, Melissa responded.

Dear Juliette,

I'm sorry that this letter has taken a long time to arrive.

So much has happened. Michael and I got married. It was a very small civil service with just our parents. A few weeks later, I had a bad accident and have been in the hospital for the past two months.

I've had multiple surgeries and the doctor says I should be fine once my rehab is over...in about 6 months from now.

I was so surprised to get your letter. A baby?? I'm happy for you.

It would be so nice to see you. Can you get away for a visit?

Let me know.

Melissa

Juliette wanted to leave immediately to see Melissa but with the B&B, she knew it wouldn't be possible. She and Marcus talked it over and both arrived at the same conclusion. This was not the time for either of them to leave, not even for a few days. Juliette wrote Melissa a heartfelt note in the hopes that she would understand. Melissa was in rehab when the letter arrived. She couldn't wait to open it to see when Juliette would be arriving. She was sure her best friend would not let her down. With excitement, she began reading.

Dear Melissa,

Congratulations!! Married? I wish I had known.

I am so sorry to hear about your accident and I hope you are feeling much better with each day that passes.

As I mentioned in prior letters, Marcus and I opened a Bed & Breakfast.

The great news is that it is flourishing, and we are packed every day. The bad news is that there is no way that I can take time off in the foreseeable future.

I am so sorry that I cannot be there for you.

Take care of yourself.

Juliette

Melissa could not believe her eyes. Throughout childhood and even throughout high school they had vowed to always be there for one another. The anger was building like a volcano about to erupt. She can't leave Marcus' side for even a brief time. We are not friends but not

anymore!

AND BABY MAKES THREE

There was no time to waste. The contractions which started just 30 minutes ago were coming faster and faster. Juliette clutched Marcus as she tried to make her way down the stairs and to the car. With each contraction she stopped and screamed out in pain. Once she was safely in the car, Marcus headed straight for I93 south. This route to the hospital was just 11 minutes from their home. He prayed he could get to the hospital before she gave birth. The contractions were now 3 minutes apart with little rest in between them.

"Hurry Marcus Hurry." The pains were like an explosion inside her body, engulfing her abdomen and back. She let out a loud scream. Suddenly she felt tremendous pressure in her rectum, "The baby is coming, the baby is coming. I have to push, Oh my God"! Marcus's heart was racing.

"We're almost there, honey. Pant, don't push. I can't drive and deliver our baby at the same time. You're doing great, it's just a few more minutes. Please don't push."

"Marcus, she screamed, hurry." He could see the hospital up ahead. Hold on Juliette. He was going 80 mph and had to make a quick turn into the entrance. He put the car in park and ran into the ER for help. A nurse and aid ran to the car with a stretcher. One look at Juliette and they knew there was no time to get her to the delivery area.

They brought her to an exam room and called the attending to deliver the baby. It happened so quickly that no-one was prepared. The ER doctor walked in the room and proceeded to don gloves. Her back was to Juliette. Juliette pushed with the next contraction and the baby was delivered into the ungloved hands of the ER nurse. It was an amazing moment for everyone.

"It's a boy", said the nurse. They quickly wrapped a warm blanket around the baby and placed him in Juliette's arms.

"A boy", said Juliette, who was smiling with the joy that only a mother could know.

"He's perfect.", said Marcus. He kissed Juliette.

"I love you.", he said. Everyone else in the room was busy with the tasks of caring for both Juliette and her newborn baby but Marcus and Juliette didn't notice. The two were mesmerized with the awe of it all. They were even more deeply in love with each other and in love with their newborn son.

Once his new family was settled in a room on the maternity floor, Marcus realized he had to leave. There was no-one looking after the B&B and they left so quickly for the hospital that none of the guests knew where they were. Juliette was about to nurse the baby which made leaving all that more difficult. He decided to stay just a while longer.

"What should we name him"? asked Marcus. They looked at their son, so beautiful, fair complexion, with blue eyes and a small amount of blond hair. For months they considered many names. They wondered if they should name him after one of their fathers or even both, but here, now, looking at him, it was clear, it was the only name that suited him......

"Jonathan", they both blurted out in unison. The surprise made them burst into laughter.

"Well, Jonathan it is," said Juliette. When she was finished nursing, Marcus took the baby from her, changed him and placed him in the nearby bassinet.

"Get some rest, he said as he leaned over to

kiss her. I love you". He kissed her again gently and left.

Juliette felt blessed to have such a loving husband and now a beautiful baby boy. What more could anyone ask for, she thought as she drifted off to sleep. By mid-afternoon Juliette felt refreshed. Jonathan slept for 4 hours which gave her some much needed rest. Marcus returned with a bouquet of white roses and yellow and blue carnations. He kissed Juliette and Jonathan then sat by her bedside.

"How is everything at the B&B?" she asked.

"Great, I got there just in time to make breakfast, eggs, bacon, toast, fresh fruit and coffee. Everyone was understanding and they are excited to see you and to meet Jonathan." He lightly brushed a finger over Jonathan's tiny hand.

"What will you serve at the tea this afternoon"?

"Muffins and scones".

"You baked"? She raised an eyebrow.

" Me bake? Of course not, silly, I'll stop by the bakery on my way to the B&B. He shook his head.

"Were you able to reach our parents"? asked Juliette.

"Yes, they are all so excited and will be here tomorrow".

"What about our friends?"

"I called everyone. Angelica is coming by tomorrow and agreed to help out at the B&B while you are in the hospital. I couldn't reach Melissa but left a message".

Juliette was pleased. Marcus had everything under control. She could relax and focus on her new baby.

In the morning Marcus arrived with blueberry scones and Juliette's favorite cup of coffee. He was always so attentive to her.

"Hey beautiful he said with a smile, making his way to her he leaned in to give her a much-anticipated kiss. I missed you" he said.

"I missed you too."

"Did you get much sleep last night"?

"Not really, Jonathan was up every 3 hours. The nurse said that this is normal especially for nursing babies. I just put him down about 20 minutes ago." Marcus walked over to the bassinet and gave Jonathan a light kiss on the head.

"I can't wait to hold him again, but I don't want to wake him."

"Trust me, he will be up soon". "So, how is everything at the B&B"?

"Great, everyone is so excited about the birth of our son, he said proudly. They can't wait to see you and him once you are released. Angelica called, she is coming later and will come to the B&B after visiting you."

"She is so sweet. What about Melissa? Did she call you back"?

"Sorry, she didn't. I also called some of our friends from the college, everyone is excited. Talk about excited, I'm surprised our parents are not here yet".

"Well, I'm glad they're not. I need to shower and feed the baby."

It was 11 O'clock and Juliette was ready to greet visitors. Jonathan finished nursing and Marcus was changing him. Jonathan was bright eyed and smiling.

"Wow, look at those big blue eyes, I hope our parents get here soon so they can see him while he is awake." The words were barely out of his mouth when they heard a tap on the door. Both sets of parents arrived together with flowers for Juliette and gifts for the baby. The room was filled with excitement and joy. They took turns holding the newborn and taking pictures. By 11:30, Angelica arrived. After saying her hello's, she picked up the baby.

"Oh, Juliette he is beautiful. I think he has your eyes." Just then the phone rang.

"Congratulations Juliette."

"Melissa, oh my God I'm so happy you called."

"Marcus left me a message that you had the baby, a boy. What's his name? tell me all about him."

"His name is Jonathan; he weighs 7 lbs. 11 oz and is 19 1/2 inches tall. You can't believe it, he is so alert, that is, when he is awake, she said with a big smile. He is holding his head up already and looking around."

"Oh, he sounds just perfect."

"He is, will you be able to come for a visit? I'd love to see you and I want you to see Jonathan."

"Sorry Juliette. I'm busy with work and can't get the time off. I'll be there in spirit." The two of them were engrossed in conversation and

Marcus didn't want to interrupt. He gave Juliette a kiss on her forehead and motioned a goodbye to her, kissed the baby and addressed Angelica.

"I'm going to the B&B for now, take your time visiting. I'll have most things done before you arrive, but you will need to prepare for the afternoon tea today and prepare things for the morning's breakfast. There are 12 guests. I hope that's not too much for you".

"Definitely not, don't worry, I'm glad to help."

Now speaking to Juliette, he whispered,

"Once she arrives, I'll be back for the rest of the day". He said his goodbyes to their parents, then kissed Juliette and Jonathan.

He returned at 4:30 pm with a surprise dinner for two, made especially for them, by Angelica. They spent an evening of quality time, fawned over Jonathan, shared a romantic dinner and planned their future.

"Do you think you'll be up to caring for the B&B now that Jonathan is here", he asked?

"Sure, I just need a couple of days to recuperate and I'll be back to my pre-pregnancy self. You'll see." She only half believed what she said. She was exhausted from all the visitors that day and was finding it hard to sleep between feedings. I'm sure this is normal, she thought. After all, women go back to work after having babies all the time.

In the morning she and Jonathan were discharged from the hospital and arrived safely at home. The B&B was filled to capacity. There was so much excitement in the air. Many of the guests wanted to join in their happiness and spend time with them and the new baby. It was wonderful and overwhelming at the same time. All she wanted to do was rest but there were so many people vying for her attention. It was late afternoon before she could take a nap. By 5 O'clock Jonathan was up and wanting to nurse. Marcus helped as much as possible but the demands on him were increasing with the number of guests arriving and departing. Angelica came by to help for a few days but had her own life. What seemed to be a dream come true was seeming more like a never-ending exhausting day relived over and over again. Both Juliette & Marcus's parents offered to stay with them but with the B&B booked solid 6 months ahead, there was no-where for them to stay. Each offered some help by staying for a few days in a nearby hotel. With the help of their parents, Juliette was able to get some much-needed sleep and the B&B ran smoothly.

In those first few months, there was little alone time for the two of them, but they didn't care. They had their son and life was wonderful.

MELISSA'S STORY

Melissa was a chubby awkward looking girl who had few friends. At an early age Melissa knew how to manipulate people without them even realizing it. Juliette was one of those people....so trusting. Melissa could get anything she wanted from Juliette. Juliette was beautiful, smart and well-liked by others but naive. They met when they were 9 years old. Melissa had just moved to New York. She was the only child of a single mother. Her father had left when she was 7, leaving a whole in her heart. She loved her father and emulated him. Unfortunately, he was not the type of person anyone should emulate. He was a con artist. Melissa learned from her father that to get anything you want you have to play the game. She watched her father talk people into all sorts of thing.... club memberships that didn't exist, subscriptions that never came in the mail and tonics that cured nothing. He was even good at manipulating her mother with his charm. In reality, he cared for no-one. It was about the game for him, the win. Each con gave him a feeling of exhilaration. Melissa would never forget the day he left. There was yelling.

"Why do you have to leave?", her mother

was shouting.

"Because that is where the money is."

"What about us"?

"I can't take you with me, especially not with a child. I'll be going place to place. I'll send money home for you both and I'll be back before you know it." She could hear her mother crying. Melissa blamed her mother for the arguments, after all, someone had to make the money. Why couldn't she understand? Melissa thought. All he wants to do is provide for us and he said he would be back soon. When Melissa woke up the next morning, he was gone. He left without saying good-bye. She blamed her mother for the argument, for not understanding.

Melissa waited for his return, but he didn't come back, no cards, no calls, not even on her birthday. She was heartbroken. Life was

hard. Her mother had to clean houses to get

money. Food was scarce and many nights,

Melissa went to bed hungry. Finally, her mother

decided to move to New York where there were

more opportunities. It was mid-summer when

they arrived and within the week Melissa's mother

was hired as a receptionist at a dental office. The

pay was good, and the hours insured she would be

home evenings, nights and weekends with

Melissa.

Many of the neighborhood children

were away with their families for summer

vacation. Melissa took a walk around the block

and noticed a girl her age jumping rope by herself.

She walked over to say hi and immediately joined

in. From that moment on Melissa made certain

that she and her new friend, Juliette, spent every possible moment together. A week before school started, Juliette's friend Angelica returned from vacation. Melissa knew that attaching herself to Juliette would ensure her being accepted by Angelica and the other classmates, and so she did. They walked to school daily and went to each other's house after school to do their homework. More often than not, they would eat dinner together. On the weekends the three girls played jump rope, hopscotch, hide and seek and when the weather kept them indoors, they would play with their Color-forms and Barbie's. They loved dressing their dolls and pretending to have the perfect life. Angelica and Juliette's dolls were clothed in tasteful clothing. Melissa on the other hand chose clothing that revealed more skin than necessary. It was a sign of who she was.

Melissa had no use for groups like the girl scouts but since Juliette was a girl scout, Melissa joined. When it came time to sell cookies, Melissa insisted that they go door to door together, telling Juliette it would be more fun that way. In reality, it insured she didn't have to do anything. Juliette sold all of the cookies, but they both received badges.

By middle school, Juliette and Angelica blossomed and always had dates for the school dances. Melissa developed acne which made her pudgy face even more unattractive. She never had a date and routinely cried about it to Juliette until Juliette invited her along. By high school, Juliette had less offers, because the boys simply did not want Melissa to come along. Melissa convinced Juliette that their friendship was more important than anyone trying to come between them and made Juliette promise that no-one would ever come between them.

College changed things. Each of the girls had different classes at different times on opposite sides of the campus. Learning came easy to Juliette and Angelica so there was always time for socializing and dating. Melissa had to study every night to barely get by. Without Juliette there to help with her homework, Melissa struggled. Juliette went to all the football games and in her second year became a sorority sister. Melissa felt lonely and missed the time she and Juliette use to spend together. Melissa no longer had a hold over Juliette, and it felt like Juliette was slipping away. All she had to look forward to, was summer vacations and winter holidays

when the friends could be together. Juliette never

missed spending time with Melissa on holidays,

that was the one thing she could always count on.

HELP IN HARD TIMES

The B&B was busier than ever with guests coming and going throughout the week. From the beginning, the new addition to their family, baby Jonathan, created quite a stir among the guests. He was an adorable baby, alert and happy. Some of the guests had stayed there often and felt more like close friends. They held him, played with him and lavished him with expensive gifts. Marcus managed all of the finances, made reservations, ordered supplies and was the designated Handy man. Juliette was in charge of housekeeping and the kitchen. Together they made a great team but had no time for one another. There was so much to do and not enough hours in the day...

By seven months of age, Jonathan was getting into everything and needed full time supervision.

"What are we going to do?", asked Juliette "yesterday he knocked over a vase filled with roses. There was water all over the sitting room carpet. Today he started to crawl up the stairs and fell. Luckily, he was only on the third step. We can't put up a gate and I can't watch him every second of every day." She was right. There was too much to do and having a baby underfoot was no way to run a business.

"What if we hire someone to watch Jonathan during the day and also help out with the housekeeping?"

"I don't know Marcus; I don't want some stranger raising our son."

"Okay, so what if we hire a full-time housekeeper, someone to clean and do the laundry, would you be willing to give that a try?"

"I think so."

It was settled. The following day Marcus advertised for a full-time housekeeper. The interviews went on for weeks. No-one seemed to be the right choice for them or their B&B; either they were too young or too old, too shy, too loud, had no references, couldn't work full time. The list went on and on. Six weeks later a lovely woman arrived for an interview. She was attractive with long honey blond hair and blue eyes, poised, well dressed, and confident. She seemed close in age to Juliette and had outstanding references, which included a governess position and light housekeeping.

"She seems like an answer to a prayer, stated Juliette. She meets all of our qualifications, except one."

"What's that?" asked Marcus.

"She's too young and did you notice how attractive she is? I'm not sure I want her around here all day every day, she said with a devilish grin."

" I didn't notice because you are the only one for me. I love you, don't ever forget that." He pulled her into his arms and kissed her with the passion of a man in love.

"It's settled then, she said with a smile... You can hire her tomorrow."

The following day, Marcus called Melanie Marsh to offer her the position. They decided to start her off part time until she was comfortable with the position. The following week, Melanie began working at the B&B four days a week. Within two weeks, she was working full time.

Melanie was a great housekeeper; she organized her day so that she had time to interact with the guests. She took the time to find out about each guest's likes and dislikes and paid attention to every detail. The guests were amazed to find their favorite chocolate on their pillows or a favorite flower lying on the bed. She was a great addition to the B&B and the clients raved about her. Marcus and Juliette were relieved to have found Melanie, they couldn't have asked for better if they ordered her from a catalog.

Melanie started each day by cleaning the top floor bedrooms working her way down to the first floor. Once the laundry was started, Melanie drove into town to find just the right special something for each of the guest. Her late morning adventures always included a visit to the Littleton Diner. She always took a seat at the counter and more often than not, ordered her favorite meal, an open roast beef sandwich with French fries and gravy followed by pie and coffee. Her bright and cheerful personality was contagious, and she commanded attention from all of the men. She seldom paid for her meal and always had a date on Friday and Saturday nights and she loved the attention.

Melanie was obsessed with her appearance. As soon as she had her paycheck in hand, she would hurry to the department store to buy a new dress, matching shoes and purse and the latest make up. Credit cards were her new best friend because she could go anywhere at any time and buy whatever her heart desired. As a result, her bills were piling up, so she was thankful for the full-time position at the B&B.

After lunch, she would return to the B&B and add her special touches to each room before helping Juliette with the afternoon tea. Melanie was amazed at Juliette's culinary skills and envied her. In fact, Melanie could barely poach an egg. After setting up the formal living room, Melanie would pour tea for each guest and inquire about their day. The men were her favorites and it didn't matter if they were single or married. She doted on them. But, if they were married, she made sure to pay extra attention to their wives. One afternoon, Timothy Moody made an offhand comment to his wife...

"Helen, he said, you should wear your hair like Melanie." Helen's face grew red.

"Excuse me, said Melanie, I think your hair looks perfect the way it is, in fact, it is stunning on you."

"tsk tsk", Melanie addressed Timothy, shaking her head in a disapproving manner. Timothy felt like a naughty schoolboy being scolded by the teacher. It was flirtatious and hot. He could feel the excitement growing as he pictured Melanie in a teacher's outfit holding a ruler and tapping it against her palm. Melanie raised an eyebrow and nodded her head in the direction of Helen. Like all naughty boys who have just been scolded, he knew what he had to do.... He apologized to Helen. Melanie gave him a satisfied smile. She knew exactly what she was doing. Helen felt validated, so much so that she didn't realize what was going on between Melanie and her husband. None of the wives did. ...everyone thought the world of Melanie.

After tea, while Juliette prepared the family's dinner, Melanie would play with Jonathan or read him a story. She was so good with him and he loved her. As Jonathan grew, they had little need for the extra help but didn't want to let Melanie go.

"Perhaps we can offer her a part time opportunity and also a great reference" said Marcus.

"I don't know Marcus. She is wonderful with Jonathan and the guests love her.... sometimes, I think they prefer her to us". And Juliette was right. Melanie had a way with the guests that no-one could top. She was gentle, kind and oh so thoughtful.

"I understand, but we don't really need the help anymore."

"You're right. When should we tell her"?

"In the morning, we'll give her time to find a new position and the references will be stellar. She'll have no problem finding another position." Juliette nodded in agreement but she was sad.

She felt close to Melanie and was

worried that she might leave entirely and cut off all future contact. Juliette waited for the right moment to explain the situation to Melanie.

"I completely understand", she said.

"You don't have to leave right away, said Juliette. Please find another position first."

Melanie put on a brave face but when alone, she couldn't help feeling hurt. After all she gave 120% to help them when they needed her. She had seen the books a few times and knew that they had the resources to pay her. Why? she asked herself. Why are they casting me aside?

With the excellent references Marcus provided it wasn't hard to find another position. Melanie kept in touch and agreed to work at the B&B during the holiday season. As hurt as she was, she knew that keeping her distance was not an option.

Even though they made the right decision, Juliette thought about all Melanie had done to make their lives easier. She thanked God for Melanie in those early years when Jonathan was getting into everything and she and Marcus were exhausted all the time. She missed Melanie more each day.

With Melanie gone and their families so far away, there was no-one there for them on a day to day basis. Most Fridays they took a few hours to drive to upstate New York so that Jonathan could spend the weekend with his grandparents. In the summer, Jonathan would spend a few weeks with his aunt and uncle and their two daughters in Connecticut. He loved those visits. It was the only time he spent with his cousins. Their home was small, which was quite a change from the Bed and Breakfast. His days were filled with swimming and the typical summer games of hide and seek, jump rope, hopscotch and kick ball. During the school year they took him on occasional day trips to the zoo, and he visited his grandparents often. Although he loved his grandparents, by age 10, he was bored when he was with them. There was nothing to do. At home he had handheld games and a mountain bike. His parents bought him whatever he wanted, whenever he wanted it. They took him to expensive restaurants, places where he met celebrities.

By comparison, his extended family was poor, and Jonathan took noticed. He had no use for people who didn't have what he had. He was spoiled, felt entitled and wanted everything his way. As the years passed, his grandparents grew older and passed away. The only family he had left, besides his parents was his aunt, uncle and cousins in Connecticut. The summer of his 13th birthday, he refused to go to his aunt and uncles house, saying there was nothing to do. In truth, he loathed their tiny home and commonness. He hated that his cousins seemed willing to settle for their poor lifestyle and couldn't understand anyone wanting to live like that. He had no use for any them. More often than not, on the rare occasion when his parents visited his aunt and uncle, Jonathan refused to go.

All of Jonathan's friends had money and enjoyed the same lavish lifestyle that he did. They were all members of the same exclusive pool and spent the summers at the pool

swimming, checking out girls and showing off by

ordering everyone fancy lunches. Marcus and

Juliette realized that Jonathan's spending was

getting out of control. They decided that they

needed to do something before he started getting

into trouble. Spending more time with him was a

must but that meant they needed more help at the

Bed and Breakfast.

It was a long shot, but they had

nothing to lose. They contacted Melanie.

Melanie who had been cast aside many years ago,

agreed to come back with the understanding that

she must work full time. She waited a long time

for this, and she wasn't going to blow it now.

Juliette and Marcus were not offering a fulltime

position, but they were so relieved that she agreed

to come back, they didn't care what terms they

had to accept. She will be an answer to a prayer,

thought Juliette, besides after all these years, she

is more like a friend than an employee, someone

who we can trust.

Jonathan was happy to have Melanie

back at the Bed and Breakfast. She was always so

kind to him and now, as a teenager, he noticed her

beauty. In fact, by the end of the first week, he

had a crush on her and would do anything she

asked, homework, cleaning his room....it didn't

matter. Her wish was his command. He

especially liked it when she got dressed to go out

for the evening. Miniskirts were his favorite. He

would sit at the bottom of the steps waiting for

her to come down, hoping to catch a glimpse of

what was under her skirt. Melanie knew exactly

what he was doing. She pretended not to notice and would intentionally stop right above his head, giving him direct access to the view he longed for. In fact, she would always ask him a question making it impossible for him to look anywhere but up. His favorite times were when he would let her know her shoelace was untied.

"Oh, my goodness, she would say, I better fix it before I trip." She would bend over ever so slowly and took her time tying her laces. He could clearly see her panties which were nearly see through. He could make out every detail. Some days she would even untie the other lace and re-tie it tighter. At first, Jonathan was embarrassed, afraid she would notice his excitement, but as time went by, he made no attempt to hide it from her. She had him tied around her finger. She knew he would do whatever she asked.

Melanie spent hours with him. They played handheld games together, she drove him to activities and sleep overs and helped him study. He loved her and loved his parents for asking her to come back.

Jonathan, under Melanie's supervision, became more of a home body. He was attentive to his schoolwork and kept his room neat and clean. Juliette and Marcus had no idea why Jonathan had changed but knew it had everything to do with Melanie. She was wonderful and they wondered how they could have ever let her go.

BABY IT'S COLD OUTSIDE

December was such a magical time of year with the snow-covered landscaping, twinkling lights and decorations throughout the town. This year was particularly cold, but Juliette and Marcus didn't care. This was their favorite time of year. For an hour each afternoon they bundled up and walked hand in hand in the fresh air. It was nice having time together, just the two of them. They talked about memories they shared, the early part of their courtship when they had to hide their relationship and how the secrecy had its own thrill.

"How would you like to spend a few days in the city?" asked Marcus.

"You mean New York"?

"Of course, New York, he replied with a chuckle, we haven't been able to go there in the past few years and we both love New York at Christmas time. We can go to Rockefeller Center and ice skate, take in a play and enjoy some much needed time away."

"What about Jonathan and the B&B"?

"Melanie can keep an eye on Jonathan and run the B&B."

"We only have a few reservations for the week of the 14th, it would be nice to get away, just the two of us", said Juliette.

"It sounds perfect." They had been to the

city several times with Jonathan. They took him to all of their favorite places and occasionally ate dinner across from stars like Frank Sinatra and Jackie Gleason. Although they were only casually introduced, and sat at different tables, Jonathan believed he shared a meal with them. Marcus and Juliette were just approaching the edge of the B&B when Juliette pushed Marcus down on the snow-covered lawn, took a leap, landing on top of him and kissed him.

"I love you Marcus...always have...always will." They kissed again. Just then Melanie was passing in front of the window and saw the two love birds. So much love and affection, she thought....and after all these years.

The holidays were approaching quickly and there was so much to be done.

Juliette and Marcus made their plans for New York, and finished decorating the B&B. Each of the guest rooms had a 4-foot Christmas tree fully decorated to match the colors in the room. Each door was adorned with a wreath and every entryway had a sprig of mistletoe. The formal living room had a 10-foot tree. It was elaborate and ornate. Each year they purchased a new ornament to commemorate that year. There were poinsettias in the formal dining room and garland tastefully placed around the fireplace mantel.

Juliette baked day and night making sure there would be enough pastries for their guests while they were away. The smell of apples, cinnamon and nutmeg wafted through the air making the B&B extra homey.

It was the 14th of December, the day

before their trip. Juliette was packing and Marcus

had just finished confirming all of the details.

Suddenly Melanie called out

"Marcus, Juliette, come quickly." She was

in the dining room. As they approached, they saw

water dropping from the ceiling. Marcus ran for a

bucket then went upstairs to find the leak. It was

coming from a guest bathroom. Marcus shut all

the water to that room and returned downstairs to

call a plumber. Distressed, he found Juliette. She

was in the dining room trying to clean up the

damage from the water. Decorations were ruined,

some of the cloth chairs were wet.

"Darling, I have more bad news. The

plumber cannot come for 2 days."

"Two days? She screeched. What are we

going to do until then"? With that she thought

about their trip. "Oh no, she said. We have to cancel our trip." But Marcus wouldn't hear of it.

"You go and take Jonathan with you. The plans have already been confirmed. I can stay here and get everything taken care of before you return."

"Marcus, this was supposcd to be <u>our time</u>" she said with disappointment.

"There will be other times, he re-assured her. I want you to go, get away for a few days. Besides, think of the fun you and Jonathan will have seeing the tree at Rockefeller Center, ice skating, and checking out all the Christmas decorations at Macy's. He's almost 14, this may be the last time you get to experience this with him. You two will have a great time, you'll see."

"I don't know Marcus; I don't feel right

about leaving you with this mess." But he wouldn't hear of it. The following day, Juliette and Jonathan left for New York.

Marcus was right. Seeing New York at Christmas, with Jonathan was wonderful. He was happy to be spending time alone with his mother. Time flew by quickly; it had been two days since they left, and they would be returning tomorrow. Juliette wanted to check in and see how things were at the B&B, but Marcus made her promise not to. He wanted her to relax and have fun. She couldn't help but wonder what was happening back at home.

Marcus barely had time to think about his family. The B&B received reservations daily. There was so much going on. Now that the leak was repaired, the men began work on the ceiling. Between the contractors and being at full

capacity, the place was chaotic. Melanie was

there by Marcus's side and made certain that all

the guests were comfy and felt like they were at

home. Marcus could not have handled everything

without her, and he was grateful.

It was late at night when Melanie

saw a light on in Marcus's office. She knocked

softly then opened the door.

"Melanie, what are you doing awake at this

hour"?

"I was just finishing up the last of the

laundry when I saw your light and thought you

might want a little sherry."

"That's very nice, come on in." She had

two glasses with her. As she took a seat, she

handed him a glass.

"Thank you for all of your help these past few days", he said.

She raised her glass.

"To hard work". He smiled and raised his glass in agreement.

"When do you expect Juliette and Jonathan home"?

"About noon tomorrow. I can't wait to see them. I miss them so much."

"I'm sure you do", said Melanie. Marcus suddenly felt the room spinning. "Wow I must really be exhausted. I'm feeling a little tipsy and haven't even finished my sherry."

"Well you have been working really hard the past few days. Finish up, you probably just need a good night's sleep. I'm sure you'll be fine, but I'll make sure you get to your room okay. I wouldn't want Juliette to come home and find her husband tripped and broke a leg or something." She gave him a half smile with a nod of her head to signify a joke. "I'll check on you as soon as I get these glasses put away." She walked Marcus to his room then made her way to the kitchen to tidy up.

She was about to get into bed when she remembered Marcus...I was supposed to check in on him. She tiptoed into his room. She could see that he had made it okay into the shower from the wet towel over the shower door. He was lying on top of the blanket with nothing more than his underwear. He is handsome, she thought and what a body. No wonder Juliette can't keep her hands off him. As she approached the bed, he looked at her. He grabbed her hand and pulled her to the bed.

"Are you coming to bed darling"?

"Coming to bed she asked"?

"Yes, I want you Juliette". She could see his maleness increasing.

"But"...

"shhhhh", he gently put a hand over her mouth then kissed her with more passion then she had ever known. She was attracted to Marcus from the start and jealous of his relationship with Juliette. She had imagined this moment over and over again and now the moment arrived. She was in his arms and he wanted her. This amazing man wanted HER. They made passionate love and fell asleep in each other's arms. As the morning sun peeked through the curtains, Marcus awoke to find himself naked in bed. The distinct aroma of intercourse could not be mistaken. What in the world? he thought. Did Juliette get home last night? He couldn't remember anything. On top of that he felt feverish.

He carefully made his way to the bathroom, showered, dressed and headed straight to the kitchen where he found Melanie cleaning up.

"Good morning, he said, where is Juliette"?

"Juliette"?

"Yes, my wife he said raising both eyebrows."

"In New York, I think. Last night you said she wasn't due back until noon and it's only 9am."

"Last night"? He asked.

"Yes, before..... she smiled shyly....you know"....

"Know what"?

"Oh, so we're pretending already."

"What are you talking about"????

"What am I talking about? How can you act like nothing happened last night?" She was getting visibly upset. Her face reddened.

"Melanie, I don't know what you are talking about. I don't remember anything about last night."

"You don't remember telling me that you love me and insisting that I get into bed with you"?

"What? No! No way"! He was horrified. His mind jumped form one thought to another. How could this be? It's a mistake...she's lying...oh my God, what have we done? His head was spinning. He had to sit down.

"You and I"? He asked.

"Yes, we made love. You held me and told me that you love me. It was magical."

"Melanie I am so sorry, I couldn't have...I wouldn't have.... I love my wife, only my wife. How can this be? The last thing I remember is getting into bed." Melanie was in tears. The pressure in her chest made it hard to breath. She quickly went to her room, grabbed her coat and left. I hate him, she thought. Anger was permeating all of her senses.

Marcus sat in disbelief. A wave of nausea swept over him. He could feel all the blood draining from his head. His hands were sweating, and his heart began to race. Another wave of nausea hit like a bolt of lightning. He was lucky to have made it to the bathroom in time. This has to be a dream, a very bad dream. I need to lie down. Crawling into bed he noticed a used condom, its contents spilling on to the sheets.

"Oh my God, Oh, my God he said over and over. What have I done? He was rambling, talking out loud. I have to clean this up before Juliette returns. What if she notices the condom in the trash? I can say it is from one of the guests. I need to air out the room."

He frantically cleaned every inch of the bedroom and bathroom, opened the windows and lit a candle. It was just before 12 noon when he finished making the bed. He shut the window, blew out the candle and went to the kitchen to make a cup of tea. He heard the car door and was riddled with shame.

FRIENDS WITH THE DEVIL

It was Melanie who returned just before Juliette was due home. Marcus greeted her calmly.

"We need to talk he said. First, let me say, I am so sorry. I never meant to hurt you. I don't know what happened to me last night, I was so exhausted, I wasn't myself. I guess that's what happens when you mix drinking with exhaustion.

Juliette and I think the world of you, and we wouldn't want to lose you. Juliette....... I don't know what I'm going to say to her. She'll never believe that neither of us intended for this to happen. She may never forgive either of us."

"Don't say anything, this will be our secret. No-one will ever need to know." She put her index finger against his lips. Outwardly she smiled but inwardly she was plotting her next move.

Wham went the car door. Marcus peered out the window.

"Their home", he said, with a sigh and went out to meet them. Marcus was relieved to see Juliette and held her tightly. Jonathan was talking incessantly about all the sights and sounds of Christmas. "I'm so happy you're back, I missed you terribly, he said. Let's agree never to take separate vacations again".

"Agreed, she said and kissed him deeply. Let's get inside, it's freezing out here."

Juliette marveled at the repairs.

"You would never know we had a leak. Thank you for taking care of everything, I know I can always trust you, she said with a smile. You're the best. I love you." His heart sank. I'm not the best, he thought, you should only know.

"Melanie, she called out. Did you have any problems while I was away"?

"Not one...Marcus was right here to help me with anything and everything I needed. We made a great team."

"I'm so glad, said Juliette, thank you for being here, I don't know what he would have done without you."

And Juliette meant every word of it. Things seemed to be running so smoothly ever since Melanie came back to the B&B. She was smart and helpful, more so than anyone could expect from an employee. But then, they never really treated her like an employee. She was more like a close family friend.

It was Thursday, one of Melanie's nights to work late but Juliette had a plan.

"Melanie, can you take Jonathan to the mall? He's meeting his friends there in half an hour. Then take the rest of the day off. Marcus and I can take care of everything here. It's my way of thanking you for taking such good care of everything while I was away."

"Sure thing. Not a problem. Come on

buddy, let's get you unpacked and off to the mall."

Jonathan happily complied, he adored Melanie.

She was always so loving towards him.

Once they were alone, Juliette said, I

think I'll do something special for Melanie to

thank her for helping you take care of everything

while I was away."

"That's nice", he said.

"You know, she said seductively, all of the

guests are out, and Melanie is gone for the rest of

the night."

"Don't you want to rest after your long

trip"?

"There is plenty of time for resting, she

said, but first I have a question for you, she said

with a wicked grin. What did you do while I was

gone"?

"What do you mean", he asked nervously.

"You know what I mean, she said raising an eyebrow while unbuttoning the top of his shirt. You didn't have anyone here to "play house" with. His hands were sweating. Does she know? He thought, or is she playing a game. His heart began to pound from fear.

Sliding one fingernail slowly across and down his chest, she gazed directly into his eyes and said,

"Were you a good boy while I was gone? How did you ever manage without me"?

Is she playing or does she know something, he thought? Shame was pouring over him.

"Pour baby all alone for several days, she continued. I can make all those lonely nights fade away. I know what you like." .... she was kissing him, seducing him. I'm worrying for nothing, he thought, after all, she is so good at seduction. He began to relax and could tell that he was getting aroused. She reached down to feel the fullness of his manhood....

"And there it is", she said with a twinkle in her eye. Shame and all, he couldn't resist her and off to the bedroom they went. Marcus loved when she played the part of a seductress. It inflamed his passion for her. No matter how many times they played that game, it always left them tremendously satisfied.

The following day Juliette took Melanie out for a day at the spa for a manicure, pedicure and massage. While they were relaxing Juliette seized the moment to develop an even more personal relationship with Melanie.

"You know Melanie, Marcus and I are so Happy to have you back with us. We really missed you when you weren't there. I've been thinking, you are more to us than an employee, you always have been. You're like one of my closest friends. It's as if I have known you forever. Do you feel the same"?

Melanie nodded. "Yes, the closest of friends." She said.

"Good! I was thinking, you never mention anything about your personal life. Are you seeing anyone"?

"Not really. I was but I don't think it is going to work out. He loves someone else."

"Are you sure"?

"Yes, he told me he loved me, and I gave into temptation. Then he said he loves someone else."

"Oh my gosh. I'm so sorry to hear it. Juliette was heartbroken for her friend. It's a shame, she said while shaking her head in disapproval, there are so many guys like that out there. We need to find you someone like Marcus. He is one of a kind."

"Yes, he is."

That night Juliette related the conversation to Marcus.

"Can you believe that guy? she said. What a slime ball. You must know someone that we can introduce her to, someone with morals"...she snarled as she thought about what Melanie told her. Marcus could barely breathe. He was ashamed before, but now he was more ashamed, horrified and sickened. How could I have done such a thing? He thought. What if Juliette finds out? What if Melanie tells her? He took a breath then responded.

"I don't think I know anyone who isn't already in a relationship, but I'll keep my eyes and ears open."

Marcus seemed different somehow, but Juliette could not put her finger on it. Marcus kept his distance from Melanie, and they did not speak unless Juliette was in the room. Marcus decided that he had to put as much distance between Melanie and himself as possible. Melanie couldn't let it go. She knocked on his office door and walked in shutting the door behind her."

"I'm pregnant, she said, and if you don't start treating me better, I will tell Juliette everything." Marcus clutched the edge of his desk. His knees went weak.

"You can't be, we used a condom. I know because I cleaned up the room myself."

"Yes, we used a condom the first time but not the second or the third."

"Second or third???? Are you kidding me"?

"Do I look like I'm kidding you"?

"What do you want Melanie?"

"For starters, I want you to open a bank account for me and our child. I want to spend some alone time with you, so you will need to find reasons for Juliette to leave for hours."

"I can't do that. I won't do that."

"Really, she said. Then I will make sure Juliette leaves for good." As she reached for the door, Marcus grabbed her arm.

"Stop. First, I want a paternity test. Then and only then will we discuss the future."

Melanie had him right where she wanted him.

The following day, Melanie was on her way into town when she noticed that she had a flat tire. She went back inside the B&B and asked Juliette if it would be alright if Marcus took her into town.

"Are you sure it's okay? I have so many errands to run. He'll be gone all afternoon."

"Of course, you have done so much for the both of us, the least I can do is let you borrow my husband for the afternoon".

On the way Marcus asked,

"How did you manage a flat tire"?

"I let some of the air out."

"Cleaver!" he said sarcastically.

They went to a doctor in another town. The ride took an hour each way. On the way there, Marcus hardly said a word, he could think of little more than the sickening thought that the paternity test might prove that he is the father.

"You should have the results tomorrow" said the doctor. The ride home was even worse. He didn't utter a word.

The call came just after 4pm.

"Mr. Donnelly"?

"Yes."

"This is Dr. Lampkin. Congratulations, you are the father."

"Marcus dropped the phone and nearly slid off the chair. Tears were streaming down his face. I need to get it together, he thought. I can't let

Juliette see me like this, what will she think? I can't let her know. I have to keep my distance.

In fact, they had been distant for the past week. He had not touched her, and she was finding it harder and harder to believe his stories of just being tired. The truth was, he was ashamed and guilty and now, his world had been turned upside down.

That evening Juliette went to bed early. Melanie, knowing this, stayed around long enough to get him alone.

"You got the results didn't you"?

"Yes. The doctor called today."

"Good, now we can plan for our future."

"Our future???? I have a wife!"

"Yes, a minor inconvenience, unless you don't cooperate. Now take your clothes off because I want you." She locked the door and stripped.

"Stop it, we can't. Juliette is upstairs."

"Yes, I know; that makes this all the more exciting. If you don't tend to my needs, I will make such a racket that not only will Juliette hear us, but all of the guests will also find out our secret."

"Fine, on one condition. After tonight, I will find time for us but only when Juliette is not around."

"Now you're getting it, she said. Let's get your clothes off." They were together and for the moment Melanie was happy. Marcus however, wanted to be sick. What was once the happiest time in his life was now a horrible nightmare.

The following day Marcus went two

cities over to open an account for Melanie. The agreement was for him to match whatever he spent on Jonathan. Marcus arrived at the B&B to find Melanie and Juliette in an intense discussion.

"May I tell Marcus"? Asked Juliette.

"I guess so", Melanie said under her breath, her body quivering like a frightened child.

"Hello darling, Juliette said to Marcus then kissed him. Melanie just told me that she is pregnant, and the father is that horrible guy I told you about, the one who used her to get what he wanted." Marcus stood in disbelief, unable to speak.

"We should track him down and make him pay."

"I think he left town said Melanie. Besides I just want to move on, for the baby's sake."

"We are here for you, aren't we Marcus? If you need anything, please ask.

In the months that followed, Marcus had frequent intimate rendezvous with Melanie. The more he was with her, the less he was with Juliette. This made Melanie happy. She was winning, which always made her happy. With no father in site, Juliette insisted that Marcus be the birth coach.

The birth was long and hard, Melanie refused to have anyone else in the birth room, except for Marcus, so Juliette had to remain outside. The moment finally arrived. It was a girl. Marcus now had a daughter.

"What will you name her" he asked?

"Marjorie, after you." Marjorie was a beautiful baby who resembled Jonathan a little.

God, I hope this is only my imagination, he thought. I hope Juliette does not pick up on it.

Melanie took a few weeks off then asked if she could bring the baby to work with her. Juliette did not think it was a good idea, but Marcus insisted, saying: "it will be fine. After all, didn't she help us with Jonathan when he was a baby"?

The baby was there each day and left with her mother each night. Juliette was so busy picking up Melanie's slack that she had little time for anything else. Jonathan liked having the baby around, he would read to her just like Melanie had read to him. Marcus wished Melanie would disappear. The blackmail was wearing on him. He had to keep up pretenses so when others were around, he and Melanie pretended that everything was fine. They worked together and shared their lives, keeping their dirty little secret.

Juliette was concerned. She had never seen Marcus so withdrawn and so pale. He hadn't touched her in weeks and seemed extra quiet.

"Marcus, I think you should see the doctor. I'm worried about you."

"I'm fine, I'm just tired."

"You have been tired before, but you have never looked so pale and haggard. You don't even want to make love, something must be wrong,"

Marcus knew things needed to change or he would lose Juliette forever. "I'm sorry honey, I have just been really tired lately. I'll tell you what, I'll get to bed early for the next few nights and if the extra sleep does not help, I'll see the doctor. Agreed"?

Agreed, she said with a much-relieved smile.

The following day, Marcus decided to stand up to Melanie. "This has to end. Juliette and I are growing apart and I don't like it. I will continue to give you money but that is it. No more intimacy. If you breathe one word of this, all of the money will stop." Melanie counted on that money, she agreed outwardly but fumed inwardly. She did not like being second best.

THE TWIST

Wham! It's was 3am., Juliette bolts upright out of a sound sleep. What was that? She wondered. The room is dark, not a sound to be heard. She shakes her head to come into full consciousness, trying to figure out what awakened her. I must have had a bad dream; she thought to herself. As she turns over, she realizes, Marcus is not there. Noticing the closed bathroom door, she sits for a moment, waiting for him to return. After a minute of complete silence, she begins to get worried and taps on the bathroom door. No answer. She calls out,

"Marcus, are you OK"? Nothing. "Marcus, Marcus", she calls out louder, but there is no response. Now frantic she opens the door.

"Oh my God, Marcus"! She turns on the light to find him is face down in a pool of blood. She rushes to him. He has a pulse, but it is faint.

"Help! someone help"! She yells as she carefully turns him over. She hears voices but does not turn around.

"Someone call 911, Marcus has fallen and is unconscious. He has a head injury and is bleeding. I can barely feel his pulse. Tell them to hurry."

Both Melanie and Jonathan we at her side trying to awaken him.

"Dad, dad, Jonathan repeated, wake up." Melanie kept her head and asked the guests who were present to leave the area and give them room and privacy.

"I'm going out front to wait for the ambulance" she said to Juliette and Jonathan who were both in a state of shock. The whirl of sirens started out as a faint sound that grew louder and louder as the rescues made their way to the entrance.

"It's Mr. Donnelly, Melanie said, he fell and hit his head, he's in a puddle of blood and unconscious."

"Where is he"?

"This way." She led the EMT's to Marcus.

"Juliette...Jonathan...what happened"? asked Bill, one of the EMT's. Bill was a good friend who had known the family ever since they moved to the area.

"Thank God you're here Bill. I don't know what happened. I heard a loud noise and found Marcus face down on the floor in a pool of blood. I felt a slight pulse then turned him to see if he was breathing. He wouldn't wake up." She was trying to be strong but broke down into tears.

"Help him Bill."

"Give us room to work."

Juliette and Jonathan stepped aside while the EMT's assessed Marcus, started an IV and hooked him up to an EKG monitor and oxygen.

"How long has it been since you found him

like this"?

"I don't really know", said Juliette. Melanie who was close by said

"It's been 12 minutes since you yelled for help." Juliette calculated the time in her mind.

"Then it must be at least 15 minutes, but I don't know how long he was hurt before I woke up and found him."

"Does he take any medications"?

"No, nothing but vitamins, what do you think is wrong with him"?

"I don't know but we are taking him to the hospital. You can meet us there".

She nodded yes. Sirens blaring, the ambulance made its way through the dark streets. Bleeeep sounded the monitor and a flat line appeared.

"No pulse, start CPR. Bill yelled to the driver, "Drive faster"! "One and two and three and four and five, breath....one and two and three and four and five, breath." This continued for 2 minutes. "Check for a pulse"

"none."

"Charge the paddles, all clear"....as the electricity went through his body, he jumped. "Nothing...charging, all clear, another bolt hit him." "Stop CPR, said Bill, he has a pulse." They continued to bag him as they approached the ER.

Juliette and Jonathan were getting ready to leave for the hospital.

"I can't drive" said Juliette.

"Don't worry, I'm here for you, said Melanie. I'll drive, I'll take care of everything."

And she did.

The ER was chaotic, there were people everywhere. A sign said write your name and take a seat. A nurse was in a small room questioning a patient. Juliette waited for the nurse to finish then quickly approached her.

"My husband was just brought in by ambulance."

"What's his name"?

"Marcus Donnelly."

"Take a seat and I will check." After a few minutes, Juliette stood up, unable to sit still any longer.

"What is taking her so long"? She blurted out, to no-one in particular. She started to pace. Jonathan tried to comfort her. He hugged her tight.

"Mom, everything is going to be OK. If there was bad news, we would have heard by now. Try to think positive." Juliette started to cry.

"I have a bad feeling about this, a really bad feeling."

"Good thoughts mom, only good thoughts." Juliette nodded her head in agreement as she tried to dismiss the doom she had felt since 3am. Out of the corner of her eye, Juliette saw the nurse and a doctor walk into the room. They approached Juliette and said,

"I have some news about our husband. Come with us." This is not good, thought Juliette. The doctor led them to a small quiet room and motioned to them to sit. Once seated, he spoke directly to Juliette.

"Your husband is still unconscious. I

ordered a CAT scan to see if there is any

bleeding. He lost a considerable amount of blood

and on the way here, his heart stopped."

Juliette shrieked,

"a heart attack? What? Why? Marcus has

always been so healthy. How can this be? How is

he? Can I see him? I want to see him." She was

frantic, almost hyperventilating.

"Mrs. Donnelly, try to stay calm. Please sit

down for a moment so that I can explain what is

happening and get some information from you

that may help your husband."

Juliette took a deep breath and sat down.

"How can I help"? she asked.

"Well, first let me say that they were able

to stabilize him in the ambulance and he is

breathing on his own now and his heart rate is

normal."

"Thank God", Juliette said under her breath.

"Now, let me ask you a few questions. Has anything like this ever happened to him before"?

"No never. As I said, he is really healthy. He has no illnesses and takes no medications."

"Are you sure he takes no medications, nothing"? The doctor looked puzzled.

"Just vitamins, why"?

"We ran a drug screen and your husband has traces of GHB in his urine".

" GHB? What's that"?

"Gamma-hydroxybutyric acid. This drug can cause amnesia, confusion, drowsiness, loss of muscle tone and respiratory failure. There are 2 similar drugs called Gamma-butyrolactone and

1,4 butanediol. They are precursors of GHB that are converted to GHB after ingestion. They are often purchased by body builders at health food stores to build muscles and burn fat."

Juliette was confused.

"This doesn't make any sense; my husband is not a body builder and is not trying to lose weight."

"Are you certain that your husband was not trying to lose weight or build muscle"?

"Yes, very certain."

"The doctor shook his head. I can think of only one other possible use and it seems unlikely."

"What is it"? asked Juliette.

"Well, GHB is a common drug used....... he hesitated, used in date rape cases."

"Date rape! She exclaimed. Who would give a middle-aged man a date rape drug"?

"As I said, it seems highly unlikely. Tell me everything you know about what happened."

Juliette recanted the story to the ER doctor. "From what you are telling me, it sounds like your husband's fall was a direct result of the drug in his system. That would also explain the shallow breathing and unconsciousness. I'll be right back."

Juliette felt like a truck hit her. Her chest was heavy, and it was hard to breath. Her head was spinning as she tried to make sense of this. Somethings not right here, she thought. Marcus appalls drugs. He would never take anything like this. She was sure of it. Then what??? Who??? How can this be? Who would do such a thing? Jonathan sat there in complete shock. He could not speak.

"I think we should call the police." said Juliette. Melanie, always calm and reassuring, spoke up.

"Juliette, don't you think you are over-reacting, after all the doctor said it is highly unlikely. Think about it, who would want to harm Marcus, let alone date rape him? I mean really"! Jonathan agreed. Melanie continued.

"As far as him taking drugs, we all know Marcus does not keep secrets and you know he would never intentionally take any drug that he thought would be harmful. So, it had to be an accident."

"What do you mean, an accident"? asked Jonathan, who finally found the strength to speak.

"Well, we have a lot of guest at the B&B.

Maybe one of them is a body builder and made himself a drink with some of this drug mixed into it."

"I guess it is possible said Juliette, but that doesn't explain how Marcus ingested the drug."

"I don't know, said Melanie, shaking her head. Grasping at straws, she tried to offer a logical explanation.

"Maybe the person needed something from his room and left the drink on the table for a few minutes. Maybe Jonathan made a similar drink and grabbed the wrong glass, I don't know...but there has to be a logical explanation."

"You know, I bet that's it, I bet whoever made the drink left briefly and somehow the glasses got switched."

"I don't know, said Juliette, her head

shaking side to side, but I have no other explanation."

"Listen, said Melanie, whatever happened had to be an accident. That's all I'm saying. We need to stay positive." Juliette and Jonathan agreed. Marcus' life was hanging in the balance; letting their minds run wild was not going to help. "Thank you, Melanie, thank you for being here and for being the voice of reason and such a good friend. I don't know what we would do without you." Juliette and Jonathan both hugged Melanie feeling grateful that she was a part of their lives.

The doctor was back with some news. "Your husband is awake. Would you like to see him"?

"Yes, can we all go in? We are all family." She smiled at Melanie.

"Sure, but only 2 at a time." Juliette and Jonathan went in first.

Marcus was awake and groggy.

"What happened", he asked?

"You collapsed in the middle of the night and hit your head. We had to call an ambulance; you gave us such a scare." Juliette started to cry. Jonathan put his arm around her shoulder.

"It's okay mom, he's going to be fine."

"Juliette, I'm sure Jonathan is right, I'm feeling stronger by the minute. He took her hand. Did the doctor say why this happened"?

"Not really, ... Well, maybe...... I don't know Marcus."

"What do you mean"?

"The doctor thinks it was drug induced."

"Drug induced? Is he crazy, I don't take

drugs? What drug"?

"Some drug used by body builders."

"What!! The exasperation in his voice was clear. He sat straight up. The shock of it all brought him to full attention. I don't understand."

"We think you may have taken it by accident. Do you remember drinking anything before coming to bed last night"?

Marcus thought. I don't remember, I don't remember. His eyes widened. He was suddenly terrified,

"I don't remember anything about last night, absolutely nothing. What's happened to me Juliette"?

"The doctor said that the drug they found in your system causes amnesia."

"I was poisoned? Who would do this to

me"? Ding ding ding the cardiac monitor alarm was loud and relentless. His heart rate was up to 140. He felt the blood drain from his head and down his body, his hands were sweating, and his face turned white. He started to lose consciousness. Just then, the nurse entered and lowered the head of his bed. She turned up the nasal O2 to 4 Liters a minute and took his vital signs again.

"Relax Mr. Donnelly, take a few slow deep breaths."

"What's happening" asked Jonathan?

"I'm not sure said the nurse, was he getting upset before the monitor started to alarm"?

"Yes, very."

"Well then, I think he had a panic attack. His vital signs are back to normal. Are you

feeling better Mr. Donnelly? He nodded yes.
Good. Would you like some water?"

"Yes", he said softly.

I don't think it is anything to be concerned about but I'm going to call his doctor. I'll be right back".

Juliette put her arms around him and held him tightly. When she let go, she said,

"I didn't mean to upset you. We have been trying to make sense of it. Melanie suggested that maybe one of the people staying with us is a body builder and made a drink with this drug in it and that you drank it by mistake."

"Why would I drink it"?

"I don't know, maybe it looked just like a drink you made for yourself. Anyway, we all know that no-one would hurt you and that everyone loves you. It had to be an accident. But let this be a lesson to all of us. With so many people coming and going, we shouldn't eat or drink anything unless we know for certain it is for us." They all agreed.

The nurse returned with Doctor Andrews.

"Take a few sips of water", she said, handing him the glass. The doctor did a quick assessment and confirmed that he did have a panic attack.

"This is very common when someone first realizes that have amnesia. It can be very frightening. You are doing well Mr. Donnelly. I think we can send you home shortly. Your wife has assured me that this had to have been an accident. Rest for the remainder of the day and be careful in the future."

"Thank you, doctor."

An hour later he was discharged and on his way home.

Juliette couldn't rest. She spoke privately to each guest. Mr. Thompson, a very muscular man, had stayed at the B&B several times. Juliette was careful in her questioning. After all, if it was an accident, she did not want to make the guest feel uncomfortable. She asked about his weight training and how he stays so muscular.

"I lift weights several times a day, eat a lot of protein packed foods and take a supplement mixed in juice each night.

"Really, she hesitated for a moment. Does it taste bad"?

"No, not at all. Actually, it has no taste, so

I have to be careful because if I forget that I already mixed it in and use more, it can hurt me. Most body builders use it but with extreme caution."

She was relieved. No-one tried to harm Marcus. It was an accident.

TRUST

Marcus was not himself. His memory of the events leading up to the collapse did not return, but he had no problem recalling the argument with Melanie and the black mail. Could she have done this? Is she evil enough to have poisoned me? He thought. Melanie had been nothing short of a saint since his hospital release. She seemed genuinely concerned about him. In fact, she doted on him day and night. But He couldn't get this out of his mind. The timing had to be more than a coincidence but he couldn't tell anyone.

The bond between Juliette and Melanie grew during this time and they were the best of friends. In a surprising turn of events, Melanie offered to move into the B&B permanently, to help Juliette run things while Marcus recuperated. At first Juliette was skeptical. How could Melanie live there and also care for her own child? Could the B&B prosper if a room was given to Melanie? But Melanie was re-assuring.

"Everything will be fine Juliette. I spoke about it with my mother and she is willing to help out with Marjorie. Marjorie can stay with my mom during the week and I will bring her here on the weekends. Since I will be living here full time, you can deduct part of the money from my pay, which should help with the loss of revenue form the room. Jonathan needs someone to drive him to activities and friends. You know how well we get along. She paused long enough to give Juliette time to think about what she was saying then she continued; I wouldn't suggest it if you had family nearby. You need to focus on Marcus right now. Another pause......I want to do this for you, for all of you. You are more than employers or even friends, honestly, to me you are family". Juliette hugged Melanie and agreed to the new arrangement.

Marcus could not believe what he was hearing. Melanie? Here 24/7. Panic washed over him. He knew if he objected Melanie would tell Juliette everything and if he didn't object, he would have to walk on eggshells day and night. This is hopeless, he thought, my life is ruined, how could I have been so stupid. He couldn't shake the feeling that this wasn't an accident, that it was Melanie, but Juliette was convinced otherwise. She believed the drug was an accident but as a precaution, she made all of the family meals herself. She vowed that there would never again be a recurrence of that dreadful night. This eased some of his fears, but he knew he had to keep his guard up.

As the months passed, Jonathan started to blossom as an older teenager. Melanie, or Meli, as Jonathan now referred to her, taught him to drive and on his 16th birthday, Marcus and Juliette bought him a brand new 941 Porsche. He was more spoiled than ever and loved showing off, driving fast with his friends and often racing them late at night. Juliette and Marcus did not approve but Melanie sided with Jonathan.

"He's a teenager, let him have fun. All of his friends race. Do you want him to be singled out, dropped from the inner circle? He's careful and they only race down by the park where there is no traffic at night."

Melanie was his champion, always siding with him and he loved her for it. Over the years, he confided in Melanie, told her things he would not tell his parent and came to her for advice. Their bond was strong, just as she planned. She had him wrapped right around her finger.

One week before Jonathan's

graduation he was hanging out at his friend's house. He was 18 and enjoying the later curfew.

At 11 O'clock the phone rang.

"It's for you bro". He was listening to the voice on the other end. His friends could see the terror on his face. The phone fell from his hand as his knees buckled. He was now on the ground, and felt lightheaded.

"What happened, what's going on"? He could hear their voices but in the distance. He was numb and couldn't speak.

"Jonathan", he could feel someone shaking him... "Jonathan what is it man"? He looked up, tears streaming down his face.

"My father's dead." There was momentary silence. Everyone was in shock.

"What, what happened"?

"I don't know. He's in the ER. I need to go there; I need to be with my mother."

"We'll drive", said one of his friends. They made it there in record time but to Jonathan, the ride felt like an hour. How can this be? He thought. He was fine before I left tonight. When he reached the ER, his mother and Melanie were waiting for him. He ran past Melanie to his mother and hugged her tight.

"Mom, how are you? Are you okay? I can't believe this. What happened"? Juliette couldn't get the words out, she was sobbing.

"Mrs. Donnelly? Juliette turned as she heard her name. "Yes"? She said between sobs.

"The doctor would like to speak with you. Come with me." Juliette held Jonathan's hand tight as they were shown to a small room.

Melanie stood there in disbelief. He doesn't even know I'm in the room, she thought, him too?? After years of being there for him, for all of them...I'm nobody, I don't even exist. Melanie was beside herself and left in a huff.

Dr. Roger's was in his mid-40's. He had been in emergency medicine for the past 10 years. He loved saving lives but dreaded the times when he had to speak to the loved ones of a patient who died. He spoke softly.

"Please sit down. Would you like something to drink"?

"Mom"? Asked Jonathan. She shook her head no.

"No, thank you", said Jonathan.

"Let me start by saying how sorry I am for your loss. Your husband suffered a massive heart attack. We tried everything but could not save him. Did your husband have heart issues"?

"No, none that we were aware of."

"Because of his age and no prior history of heart disease, we will need to perform an autopsy. The nurse will bring in the consent forms. Do you know if your husband is an organ donor"?

"I believe so. I can't talk about this anymore. Can we see him"?

"Certainly." Dr. Rogers brought them to the bedside.

It was hard to see his lifeless body with all of the tubes and wires hooked up to machines. Juliette broke down, she was wailing as she clung to Marcus. Jonathan felt like the room was closing in on him, but he had to be strong for his mother.

As they were leaving the hospital, they remembered Melanie and looked for her. She was no-where in sight.

Melanie was at the B&B when they returned.

"I'm so sorry" she said as they entered. Both Juliette and Jonathan hugged Melanie. "Would you like something to eat? I made sandwiches"?

"No thank you, it's been a long night said Jonathan, we should try to get some rest. Melanie, he added, we would appreciate it if you could look after everything here. My mother is in no condition to run the B&B right now."

"Of course, don't worry about anything. I have it all covered".

Word got out the following day.

Angelica was heartbroken when she heard the news. She and Genaro moved to Australia a few years prior but she always kept in touch. Both Angelica and Juliette looked forward to their weekly phone calls, letters and the family photo's they would send each other. Angelica wished she could be there for Juliette, but she just couldn't leave. Melissa routinely corresponded by mail, something that had been going on since Melissa's accident so many years ago. Hearing from her two oldest and dearest friends always brought a smile to her face. Their letters gave her comfort and joy, but not now. Now, there was no joy to be found.

TIME OFF WITH PAY

Melanie had been running everything for months. She was given free reign with ordering supplies, paying all the bills and balancing the books. Juliette was in a state of depression and was of little help. It was up to Melanie and Jonathan to run everything. Jonathan offered to take over the financial responsibilities, but Melanie reassured him that she was on top of it and that she enjoyed it.

"No worries, she said...I have everything under control, and everything is going according to plan". What a relief. Thought Jonathan. Thank God for Melanie, I couldn't survive this without her.

Jonathan hadn't seen his friends in months. The days of the carefree teenager were long gone. He had planned on going to college with his friends, but he was busy with the Bed and Breakfast and caring for his mother. He considered calling his aunt and uncle in Connecticut but couldn't bring himself to swallow his pride. After all, he was the one who stayed away all those years and looked down on them.

Juliette was not the same since Marcus' death. One day ran into another. Weeks turned into months and months into years. It was two years since Marcus died and Juliette had not come to terms with it. Her grief was overtaking her mind. She ached in her soul and cried herself to sleep night after night. She hardly ate and rarely slept more than a few hours. She no longer cooked and wanted to be by herself. She spent her days looking at pictures of her, Marcus and Jonathan. They were so happy once, but the more she thought about the happiness they shared the more despondent she became. She missed Marcus and wanted to be with him.

It was 3am when she decided that she had to explain things to Jonathan. She hoped he would understand.

The next morning when Jonathan woke up, he noticed an envelope on his bedroom floor. He opened it and was frozen by its contents.

My Dearest Son

I love you more than you can imagine, and I hope you can understand why I had to do this.

Please do not try to save me. It will be too late, and I am in a better place.

I am with your father now and we will see you again. I know you are sad, but I could not go on.

Have a good life my son and take care of yourself.

Your loving mother

Jonathan could not believe what he was reading. He ran to his mother's room. She was gone, icy cold with an empty bottle of pills on the bed. Jonathan collapsed just as Melanie was walking by. She entered the room and quickly realized what happened. She called 911 and shook Jonathan.

"Please wake up" she said. Jonathan's eyes opened.

"What happened, where am I"? He was dazed.

"You're in your mother's room." With that his heart began to race. He was panting trying to catch his breath. The sirens were blaring and now the room was filled with Fire Fighters, police and EMS. They sedated Jonathan who was overwhelmed with his mother taking her own life and transported him to the hospital of observation.

"Are you alright miss" they asked Melanie.

"Yes, I think so. I'm just in shock. I can't believe she would do this." Then the questions started.... Who was here last night? Where were you when it happened? Does she have any enemies? What was her behavior like? How was her relationship with her son? Melanie couldn't believe it. It was clearly a suicide, after all, there was a note and there was never even an argument between any of them.

The Bed and Breakfast was closed for four weeks following Juliette's death. There was yellow tape across the door. It was considered a crime scene until proving otherwise. In the weeks that followed, the police ruled Juliette's death a suicide. Jonathan was slowly coming to terms with everything and was able to help out with the Bed and Breakfast. He felt so alone. At least I have Melanie, he thought.

Winter was almost over, and

Melanie wanted some time off.

"I'd like to take a week off, she told Jonathan. I know it will be difficult but I have all of the finances in order so all you really need to worry about are the day to day things, you know, reservations, cleaning rooms, laundry, breakfast and the afternoon tea. You don't have to make anything fancy. You can always put out cookies from the bakery.

"I'm sure I can manage, he said. You have been a wonderful help. Actually, you have gone above and beyond. Is one week enough"?

"Yes, she smiled. I'll leave next Saturday for 1 week".

Melanie made sure she took care of all of everything before leaving. She double and triple checked every detail on her list. She was relieved that everything was in order and looked

forward to morning when she would leave for a

much needed vacation.

ONE SPRING DAY

It was such a beautiful day. Spring had finally arrived. The warmth from the sun shone through the front parlor and the foyer. Jonathan opened the large front windows. He could smell the familiar scent of watermelon which was a sign that someone nearby just mowed their lawn. He took a deep breath and smiled. Both of his parents loved the fall, but for Jonathan, there was nothing like the sights and smells of spring. The week had passed quickly and Jonathan eagerly awaited Melanie's return. He didn't realize how much extra work there would be with her gone. He wanted to do something special to show his appreciation and to welcome her home. After all, this was her home. They were close since his youth and now with both of his parents gone, she was all the family he had.

He had a thought and quickly took a walk to the garden. Spring had indeed arrived. There was an array of brightly colored flowers in full bloom. Melanie loves fresh flowers. This will be a wonderful welcome home for her. He arranged the flowers in 2 different vases and placed one in the front parlor, where she would see it as soon as she stepped inside. The other he placed on the bureau in her bedroom with a handwritten note that said:

Dear Melanie,

Thank you for everything and welcome home.

I truly appreciate you.

Love,

Jonathan

After everyone finished breakfast, he hurried to complete the daily chores. He checked his watch, it was nearly 1pm. Hmmm he thought. Melanie should have been back by now. Oh well, I'm sure she'll be here any minutes. He decided to wait on the front porch taking in the scenery and getting his fill of springtime air. He rocked back and forth, relaxing with each breath. The past few months had been the most difficult ones of his young life, but he had stepped up, had become a man. His parents would have been so proud of him, he thought, as he drifted off to sleep.

It was a car door closing that startled him. Finally, he thought, excited to see Melanie.

"Hi Jonathan".

"Mr and Mrs Vitali, welcome back". They weren't due until late afternoon. He peered at his watch as he went to get their luggage. 4pm? I must have been more tired than I thought. Melanie must be inside getting everything ready for afternoon tea. She is always so considerate.

After checking in the Vitali's and showing them to their room, he went to find Melanie. She was no-where to be found. The kitchen was dark and the parlor empty. Nothing had been set up for the guests. He hurried to get everything ready. Panic was starting to hit him. He went to her room and knocked on the door. No answer. He knocked harder and harder before opening the door. It was then that he noticed the missing picture. He had not been in Melanie's room before but a few times she had left the door open and he had noticed the baby picture of her daughter hanging on the wall next to her bed. Now, the room seemed cold and empty. How did I miss this when I set the flowers down this morning? With trembling, he went to the closet and opened the door. "Oh my GOD"! He shrieked. The closet was empty. He opened the drawers to the bureau. Everything was gone. There was nothing, nothing to indicate that anyone was ever in this room. A sea of emotions flooded his brain...fear, shock, sadness,

frustration, confusion and anger. How could she

do this? Why would she do this? Why would she

leave without a word? She was like a second

mother to me.

He thought about calling the police, but

what would he say to them, an employee had

walked out without a word? He called the

emergency contact number that Melanie had

given when she first arrived. The number had

been disconnected. He felt sick and had to sit

down. What am I going to do? I can't run the

B&B alone. He could hear the chatter from the

parlor and realized that he had to shake this off

and tend to the guests. It was all he could do to

smile. The guests were asking about Melanie.

They expected her back today.

"She said she needed some extra time with her daughter" he said, which seemed to satisfy everyone, everyone except Jonathan.

It was nearly midnight when he finished everything that needed to be done for the day. He was exhausted from the work and drained from all the emotions he was feeling. It had been a horrible few years. First with the death of his father then his mother's sadness, the suicide and now this. He felt completely alone, small and insignificant. He wondered how he could get by, how he could even face another day. He needed help if he wanted to keep the B&B afloat but who could he trust......No-one, that's who, No-one, he thought, but I have no choice, tomorrow I'll place a help wanted ad in the paper,

RICHES TO RAGS

He was setting up breakfast for the guests when the knocking began. It was 8am. Jonathan hurried to the door. There were nine strong looking men on the front porch. Behind them he could see several moving trucks lining the curb of the B&B. "Can I help you"? He asked.

"Yes, responded the guy nearest to him." There was no doubt that he was the man in charge. He was huge and intimidating.

"We have orders to seize all of your assets. Here is the paperwork".

"Seize my assets" What? Is this a joke."

"No, it is not a joke" said the man as he handed Jonathan the legal documents.

"How? Why"? Jonathan's head was spinning.

"Please step aside sir."

Jonathan pulled himself together to muster all the strength he could, then responded with an emphatic "NO. You must have the wrong place."

"Are you Jonathan Donnelly"? The man asked.

"Yes."

"Then there is no mistake. Now step aside."

"Who are you anyway and what is going on? The only debt we have is the mortgage on this property and that is paid monthly and ahead. You are out of your mind if you think I'm going to allow any of you to even step foot inside." With that he slammed the door shut. Some of the guests heard the commotion and hurried to see what was going on.

"Are you okay Jonathan"? The color had completely drained from his face.

"I don't know he said. I don't know what is going on. These men showed up and said they are here to take all the furniture. How can that be? The furniture is paid for and we have no debts." One of the guests asked to see the document that Jonathan was holding.

"Jonathan, it says they can take the

furniture as partial payment for debts owed. You better call a lawyer." The words were still hanging in the air as the sound of sirens came closer and closer. A police car stopped in front of the B&B. Two officers approached the door and knocked. Jonathan opened the door. "Officers I'm glad you're here. Please come in."

As they stepped inside, one of the officers said, "Mr. Donnelly, the men outside have a court order to remove all furnishings. You need to let them in. If you don't, we will have to arrest you."

"How can this be? I don't understand. No-one ever said that we owed money. I was never contacted. How can there be a court order to take everything"? "I don't know the details Mr. Donnelly but I have seen the court order and it is real."

"But I have guests here.

"You will have to refund their money so they can leave. I'm sorry but please step aside." Jonathan waved a hand as if to surrender then went to his guests to try to explain why they had to leave. As all the guests scurried to pack their things, Jonathan sat down. Both officers could see the confusion on his face. In situations like this people typically try to lie their way out of it, but there was something compelling about his body language. They believed him. At least they believed he had no knowledge as to what was going on. They decided to probe.

"Jonathan, one officer began, what exactly is your roll in the B&B"?

"I own it. My parents passed away and I inherited it from them.

"How long ago was that"?

"A few months ago, why"?

"I'm just wondering. Who else works here? Jonathan remembered that Melanie left. "Up until a week ago, Melanie Marsh was here. She took care of most of the day to day things."

"What happened a week ago? Was she fired"?

"No, she asked for a week off. She was due back yesterday but never showed up. I checked her room and all of her belongings are gone. First that and now this."

The officers became suspicious. "Do you personally handle the financial end of the business"?

"No, I mean I guess I have to now. Ever since my father passed away, Melanie took care of all of the finances."

"Melanie"?

"Yes, why? You don't think she...... It can't be. Melanie was like part of the family. She helped raise me. She was there for me when my parents died. It can't be."

"We're not accusing anyone we are just trying to help you. May we look around"? Jonathan waved a hand to indicate go ahead.

"Which room belonged to Melanie"?

"Third floor, second room on the right but you won't find anything. As I said, she left nothing. You don't mind if we check"?

"No, go ahead."

"Mr. Donnelly, I suggest you call the bank and verify funds in the business account and also any other accounts.

The police could hear retching. It was Jonathan, he had just spoken with the bank manager. He was on the floor, hyperventilation with the dry heaves.

"This is officer Nolan, dispatch an ambulance to this location. I have a male in his late 20's hyperventilation with the dry heaves. He is suffering from shocking news he just received.

"Jonathan, the other office said calmly, look at me and do as I do, try to slow your breathing, take a deep breath."

"I can't", he was now gasping.

"Listen to me Jonathan, you are going to be fine. Help is on the way."

"Oh my God, Oh, my God, what am I going to do? He was hysterical. There is nothing left, ahuh, ahuh, ahuh, nothing, ahuh, not a penny in the account." He was gasping. Then suddenly fainted. The EMT's arrived to find him unconscious on the floor. They set up an EKG and gave him oxygen.

"Jonathan can you here me." He woke up surrounded by EMT's and the two police officers.

"What happened"?

"You had a panic attack and hyperventilated until you passed out. How are you feeling"?

"Numb, exhausted."

"We gave you something to calm you. You should try to get some rest." Rest? he thought. Rest where?

By late afternoon everyone was gone along with everything he owned, furniture, paintings, knick knacks, dishes, pots and pans, flatware, the actual silverware his parents were given as a wedding gift, all his mother's jewelry, his clothing, everything. Thank God they didn't take the food. At least this would get him by in the short term. Other than that, he had nothing left except the clothes on his back and a few hundred dollars in his wallet. The following day, his car was repossessed.

It had been a month and the police were no closer to finding Melanie. The detective on the case asked to search the house again.

"Why? The officers who were first here didn't find anything."

"We are hoping Mr. Donnelly, hoping to find a clue as to the whereabouts of Melanie Marsh."

"Go ahead, do what you want, there's

nothing here. For the past month, Jonathan spent his days lying on a twin bed in front of a small TV eating junk food and whatever else he could find. The electric had been turned off, the B&B provided little more than shelter. He knew he needed a job but could not bring himself to apply.

"Mr. Donnelly, said the detective, we are heading out."

"Did you find anything"?

"No, but we will keep trying." The officers were trying to stay positive, but the truth was that they were no closer to finding Melanie than they were a month ago.

By late November, the police had given up and closed the case. Jonathan's funds were depleted, the bank seized the B&B. With no-one to turn to, he was left homeless and living on the street.

It was so cold at this time of year and there was snow and ice on the ground. He tried to get warm but couldn't. He felt feverish and was coughing more each day. He tried to make a tent out of trash bags but that gave him little protection from the icy temperatures. He just couldn't believe it. He once had everything and now look at him, he was freezing to death, starving and alone. There was no-one there for him. No-one cared.

A NEW BEGINNING

November 1995

"So, that's my story, said Jonathan. I still

can't believe it. It seems like a bad dream, a

nightmare actually. How could I have been so

blind? My parents too...was she so cleaver, such

a great actress that we all bought into her

pretense." Sara, sat still, as if frozen. She had no

words. What do you say to someone who has

been though all of this? How do you help? Can you help? How can I help? she wondered.

"Jonathan, can't the police do more"?

"They have nothing to go on. They suggested I get an attorney, that is, if they can find her. An attorney, right! I don't have a penny to my name. I'm living on the street like an animal."

"What about family? Do you have any family that can help you"? My grandparents passed away when I was in my early teens." I have one aunt and uncle and their two daughters but years ago I stopped all contact with them. I was selfish and refused to have anything to do with them. I can't call them now."

Sara was thinking, taking it all in. She was intelligent and had a keen mind. She should have been a detective. There was

something that played over and over in her mind.

With both sets of grandparents gone, how could

he be left with nothing?

"Jonathan, you said that all of your

grandparents passed away when you were in your

early teens, right"?

"Yes."

"Well, I was thinking, when something is

bequeathed to a minor, it is placed in a trust until

they reach adulthood. Did your parents ever say

anything about your grandparents will? I mean,

it's just a thought but maybe they left you

something."

"I don't know, said Jonathan. I doubt my

parents would keep something like that from me."

Jonathan was intrigued and pensive.

"No, it's not possible." He seemed a bit agitated.

"I didn't mean to upset you, said Sara. I'm sorry. Actually, I need to get to work. Would it be okay if I stop back later"?

Jonathan gave a slight affirming nod...

"sure, I'm not going anywhere". Sara couldn't stop thinking about Jonathan and his situation. What if...she wondered. What if......

Sara loved her job and loved the people she worked with. She was a senior law student doing her internship at one of the largest and certainly most prestigious law firms in New Hampshire. As she entered the building on Main street, she smiled. She felt more at home here than any other place on earth. Helping people is what she lives for and the attorneys here went out of their way to help those in need. She knew they did pro bono work for people in need and Jonathan Donnelly, was definitely in need. She tapped on the opened door of one of the partners.

"Come in Sara". Sara had a great relationship with all the attorneys in the firm. She was a hard worker and conscientious. They liked her work ethics and they planned on hiring her full time after graduation.

"What's up"? Asked the senior partner, Jeff Stone. Sara confided everything to Jeff.

"I think he has a case and I'm wondering if you can help him." Jeff sat for a moment thinking about everything she had told him.

"Do you think this guy is on the up and up"?

"Yes, my gut tells me he is for real."

"Well, said Jeff. I think there is more than one case here."

"You mean you will take on his case pro bono"?

"Yes, with you as my assistant. It will mean long hours without extra pay. Are you in agreement"?

"Yes, of course, thank you Mr. Stone, thank you.

Let's get our investigator involved. Have him look into the wills of the parents and grandparents as well as Melanie Marsh."

"Right away", said Sara. As she left his office, she sighed a sigh of relief. What if she is right? What if.........

SECRETS KEPT

The firm's investigator, Dylan Himes was top notch and left no stone unturned. He was very good at finding people who didn't want to be found. There was no record of anyone with the name Melanie Marsh. He went to the Bed and Breakfast for clues. There was a foreclosure sign on the door and the building was empty. He picked the lock and went inside. Other than a few cobwebs, he saw nothing. Room by room he checked for clues but found nothing except for a box of memorabilia in the foyer. There had to be something he missed, there had to be. He methodically checked each room again. Under his right foot, he felt a floorboard give way slightly in one of the upstairs bedrooms. He lifted the board and there to his surprise was a large bag of unopened mail. I'm sure the clue to Melanie Marsh is somewhere in this bag, he thought to himself. Satisfied, he took the box of memorabilia and the bag, locked up and headed back to his office.

Late notice, late notice, late notice; they were all the same. Then he stumbled upon it, an odd-looking pink envelope with a scalloped edge. He opened it quickly. Inside was a letter that read:

> *Dear Jonathan,*
>
> *It's too bad that you got caught up in this.*
>
> *Unfortunately, you're getting hurt*
>
> *was a necessity that could not be*
>
> *avoided. I finally got even.*
>
> *Now I can stop pretending.*
>
> *By the way, my name is not Melanie*

Marsh. It's Melissa Bryant.

No wonder there was no record of a Melanie Marsh. Melissa Bryant? So who is Melissa Bryant and why was she pretending to be someone else? At the bottom of the box he found Juliette's high school yearbook. Let's see if you are in here, he muddled to himself. Sure enough, Melissa Bryant was in the yearbook. She graduated with Juliette. He did a double take.

This can't be? He scratched his head and looked again. Melissa Bryant is unattractive with straight brown hair and brown eyes. Melanie is beautiful with wavy honey blond hair and blue eyes. She's beautiful and they look nothing alike. What in the world? he thought.

Early in the investigation he found an M. Marsh who owned a home in California but when he called the phone number, an elderly man who answered said he never heard of anyone by the name of Melanie Marsh. Dylan Himes was perplexed. A clue is a clue, he said to himself. By late afternoon he was on a plane to California. The following morning, he was at the home of Martin Marsh. Knock, knock.....

Martin Marsh wasn't as old as he sounded over the phone. Parkinson's has taken

over his body and his voice. The tremors were
constant. "Can I help you"? He asked. Mr.
Marsh, "I'm Dylan Himes, I called you recently
asking about a Melanie Marsh."

"Yes, I remember but I told you I don't
know her. What is this about"?

"I'm a private investigator. He showed him
his credentials. May I come in for a moment"?
Martin was hesitant but motioned him in. Dylan
took out two pictures, one of Melissa and one of
Melanie. "Do you know either of these woman"?

"Yes, that's my son's ex-wife, Melissa".

"Do you mean Melissa Bryant"?

"Yes, Melissa Bryant Marsh. The surgery
turned her into a real beauty, don't you think?
Too bad it didn't help her personality. She was a
hand full before the accident, but after the

accident,...... a real nut job. Thank God my son divorced her."

"When did she have plastic surgery"?

"After the accident. Her entire face was deformed beyond recognition. After the plastic surgery, she decided that she wanted an entire transformation, changed her hair color, got colored contacts and went to the gym every day...but nothing helped, nothing made her happy. I haven't seen or heard from her in years. Last I heard she went home to live with her mother".

"Do you know where that might be"? "I'm not sure but I think New Hampshire. Is she in some kind of trouble"?

"Trouble is an understatement. Where can I find your son"?

Michael was a plastic surgeon in

private practice and had a home near his fathers.

Dylan waited outside Michael's residence.

Finally, a car pulled in the driveway. Dylan

approached as the man exited the car.

"Excuse me, are you Dr. Michael Marsh"?

"Yes, and who are you"?

"Dylan IIimcs, I'm a private investigator

for a law firm. I want to ask you a few questions

about your ex-wife".

"God help me, just the thought of her

makes the hair on my neck stand up". All of the

drama and frustration flooded his mind. All the

times she flew off the handle over nothing, the

vase she threw across the room in a rage...it was

his grandmother's, the only thing he had left of

her and Melissa knew that. Then there was the

time she flushed the vintage earrings, he gave her

as a birthday gift, down the toilet because he didn't compliment her dress. The overspending, the messy house and what frightened him the most was that she never showed an ounce of remorse.

"Please come inside where we can talk privately". "So how can I help you Mr. Himes"?

"I'm trying to find Melissa. Have you heard from her in the past few months"?

"No, I haven't heard from her in years. I have a restraining order against her".

"Would you happen to have any ideas on where she might be"?

"As I said, I have no contact with her. She had a place in Monrovia after the divorce, but I thought she rented it out when she moved back home with her mother. I can give you the addresses, but I have no idea if she still lives there."

"That would be helpful and just to be certain, can you look at these photos and let me know if they are your ex-wife"? Dylan handed the photos to Michael.

"Yes, that is Melissa before the accident and this one is after the reconstruction".

"What was her maiden name"?

"Bryant".

"Michael, do you know Juliette Lang Donnelly"?

"I don't actually know her...I never met her. I was invited to her wedding but could not get away. Melissa was so excited to go but came home in a bad mood. She and Juliette were best friends from grade school, but the way Melissa spoke about her made me cringe".

"What do you mean"? She was jealous of Juliette's relationship. She felt like Juliette had abandoned her. You could hear the hatred in her voice as soon as she mentioned Juliette. In fact, the hatred escalated after the accident. Melissa wanted Juliette nearby, but Juliette had just given birth and couldn't come to California. Melissa needed to be the center of attention and Juliette had her new baby. That infuriated Melissa. Once I heard her saying, under her breath, I'll get even one day".

"So, what happened after that"?

"I couldn't take it anymore. At first, our relationship was good but once we got married, Melissa's suffocating personality began to show through, and it was too much for me. She

couldn't manipulate me which seemed to increase

the daily arguments. I knew I had to get away

from her. The day I told her that I filed for

divorce, she stormed off and was so enraged that

she caused a head on collision. It took her months

to recover from the multiple broken bones and the

plastic surgery to repair her deformed face. While

she was in rehab, the divorce was finalized. I

know she contacted Juliette while she was

recovering and asked her to come to California.

When Juliette said no, Melissa wanted nothing

more to do with her. That's all I know."

"Thank you, Dr. Marsh, for the information

and the addresses. You have been very helpful.

He handed him a business card. Please let me

know if you hear from Melissa. I'll be on my

way. Thank you again for your time." Dylan had

enough to go on. Now he needed to actually find

Melissa. He would start with her last known

address and then find her mother.

Over the next few days Dylan was

on a stake out. He patiently observed the last

known address of Melissa Marsh. On the third

day a package was delivered and left by the front

door. Half an hour later, a neighbor walked up to

retrieve it.

"Excuse me, he said. Are you a friend of

Melissa Marsh"?

"Who's asking"?

"I'm Dylan Himes, a private investigator

for a law firm." He handed her a card. "So, are

you a friend of Ms. Marsh"?

"A neighbor. Melissa asked me to take in

her mail and any packages while she was away".

"Away where"? "I'm not sure. All I know
is she went to see her mother. She has rented this
place for the last 20 years. The tenants left about
a month ago and she will be moving in, I think
next week."

"Please let me know when you hear from
her or when she returns, whichever happens first."

"Should I be concerned"? Not at this time
but do not mention that I was here."

Dylan reported back to the partners
at the firm who immediately notified the police.
Before long Melissa Marsh would be in custody.

JUSTICE FOR ALL

Within the week, the police found Melissa
Bryant AKA Melanie Marsh. She was arrested
and plead guilty of embezzlement. Melissa's
belongings were searched. In Melissa's wallet
there was a picture of a young teenage girl who,
for some strange reason, looked very familiar.
Dylan Himes went to the jail to see Melissa.
"Who is this girl"? He asked.

"That's my daughter. Where did you get it"?

"I got it from your belongings. It was in your wallet. Where is she now"?

"She is with her grandmother."

"Your mother"?

"Yes".

"Where are they"?

"I'd rather not say. She has nothing to do with this".

Further investigation found the child living in Colorado with her grandmother. Court ordered DNA testing determined that Melissa's daughter is Jonathan's half-sister. Jonathan was stunned. How could his father cheat on his mother? It didn't make sense. He loved her. They were completely in love with one another.

The investigator showed him a picture of the little girl. "She looks like she is about 14" said Jonathan.

"Yes, she will be 15 in September."

Jonathan thought about that time in his life 15 years ago. That was the year Melanie encouraged his mother to take him to NY. It was also the time when his father was first hospitalized for an unexplained reason. After confirming all dates, Jonathan asked the police to look into the untimely deaths of his parents.

The police started by questioning Melissa. Melissa couldn't help but tell everyone what she did and how she did it. She had the upper hand, she got her revenge and knowing this gave her great joy. At her sentencing she walked the judge through the entire process.

"I was always unattractive, and Juliette was always beautiful. We were the best of friends until Marcus came along. Once they were a couple, there was no more room in Juliette life for me, so I moved out of state to start a new life. I met Michael. We dated for a few months then got engaged and married. Everything seemed to be going well until Michael selfishly filed for divorce. I was involved in an auto accident. It left me severely disfigured. After multiple plastic surgeries, I was beautiful for the first time in my life. There was no resemblance to my old appearance. I dieted, changed the color of her hair and got colored contacts. It was the new me, a beautiful, vibrant sexy me and I was going to get anything and anyone I wanted.

I decided to keep in touch with

Angelica and Juliette by mail only and never told them about my appearance. knowing that Juliette was hiring at the B&B, it was my best opportunity to get revenge. I applied for the job at the B&B and was hired. They had no idea it was me. I fooled everyone, which satisfied me for a while. ...but then I had to watch the lovebirds day in and day out. Half the time they didn't even know I was there.

When Juliette took Jonathan to the city during the Christmas holiday, I slipped a pill into Marcus's drink, the pill ensured we would be together. He made love to me that night. Even though he called out Juliette's name, he was with me and it was wonderful. In the morning he didn't even remember. He was angry when he found out we slept together. All he could think about was Juliette and her feelings, not mine. I'll

never forget his words "Juliette will never forgive

us"...well, duh, that's the point isn't it. But

Marcus didn't want me, he wanted Juliette. It was

always Juliette even when he found out I was

pregnant with his child. I was pissed!!! If I

couldn't have him all to myself, neither would

she. I blackmailed him into continuing our sexual

relationship. But one day he refused to continue

the relationship, so I drugged him again, this time

giving him too much. He was never the same and

died soon after. With Marcus out of the way, I

had one more obstacle to my happiness. I got

closer and closer to the grieving Juliette and I

doted on Jonathan. It took a while but eventually,

I convinced Juliette to turn over control of the

B&B to me, including the finances. It was so easy

to destroy her. She was always an easy

mark...even when we were children.

When she wanted to get up and spend

time with Jonathan. I would slip her a pill which

made her dizzy. I added drugs that would cause

depression and reminded her daily of how much

she couldn't go on without Marcus. She finally

died of a broken heart, or maybe from the pills.

Who knows....I left a suicide note for good

measure. This cleared the way for the final blow,

.... complete destruction of everything Juliette and

Marcus had, including their son.

Jonathan couldn't believe what he

was hearing. He and his mother and father loved

Melanie and trusted her. What a monster! he

thought. He felt the blood draining from his head.

He grabbed the edge of his seat and took a deep

breath. He wouldn't give her the satisfaction of showing his true feelings. She sat there with a smirk on her face and it took everything he had in him not to slap it off. Within minutes the judge made his ruling and ordered her to be remanded to a psychiatric institution for the rest of her life.

Mrs. Bryant, Melissa's mother, was in the courtroom. Like Jonathan, she couldn't believe what she was hearing. Did she know her daughter at all? Thank God my granddaughter is not here today, she thought. Mrs. Bryant started to shake uncontrollably and began crying hysterically. She couldn't believe all the horrible things Melissa had done. This was her only daughter and she was in shock. To compound things, she felt strangely responsible for all the pain and suffering that Jonathan and his family had gone through at the hand of her daughter.

Melissa had given her a substantial amount of money a few months ago saying she had hit the lottery. Now, the truth was hitting her, and she knew what she had to do. The courtroom was empty except for Mrs. Bryant, Jonathan and Jonathan's lawyer. Mrs. Bryant approached Jonathan.

"I'm so sorry Jonathan. I don't understand this, I don't understand how my daughter could have done this. I know this doesn't change what she has done or take away your pain, but Melissa gave me money a few months ago and I am going to give it to you. Can I meet you tomorrow"?

Jonathan was in shock, first by Melissa's testimony and now this. He took a moment to reply. "Yes, I can meet you. I understand that your granddaughter is my half-sister."

"What? She sank into the chair opposite
Jonathan. I didn't know". I'm sorry."

"I would like to meet her."

The following day they met for lunch.
Marjorie, his father's daughter, his half-sister was
there. He had remembered meeting her when she
was very young and she remembered him and
how he read to her and played dominos with her.
She liked him back then but now they were virtual
strangers meeting again under a horrible
circumstance.

"You have our father's eye" he said. A tear
ran down her cheek.

"I'm sorry, I didn't mean to make you cry."

"No, it's not you and it's nothing you said.
I'm just sad that I never really knew him."

Jonathan realized that he was not the only one hurting, in fact all three of them had been victims. This reality actually eased his pain. He realized he was not alone. In an odd turn of events, these two people were his family.

Mrs. Bryant handed Jonathan a check. The money she gave him was enough to get him back on his feet. He was able to secure an apartment, a car and everything he needed to live comfortably. A nearby B&B was looking for a manager and Jonathan was hired immediately. He had been wondering how he could turn this horrible situation around. How he could make his parents proud? That was a mystery, but he decided to make the most of every day.

A few months later, Sara, with the help of the lawyers at the firm, located a trust that had been put away for Jonathan. He and Sara had spent so much time together over the past few months, that not only did he feel indebted to her, but he liked her. They had common interests and made each other laugh. He felt comfortable with her and she with him. In the spring of the following year, everything fell into place. Jonathan was able to buy back the B&B. He and Sara began dating and he and Marjorie had each other. Most importantly, he was learning to trust again. Through this tragedy, Jonathan learned life's biggest lesson, when you love money more than others, you have nothing.

ABOUT THE AUTHOR

Geralyn Vilar is a mother and grandmother. She lives with her husband, David, in The Villages, Florida and enjoys singing, dancing, cooking and of course, writing.

This is her first novel.

Made in USA - North Chelmsford, MA
1056467_9798622234521
03.19.2020 1833